Bruno Fólner's Last Tango

Bruno Fólner's Last Tango

Mempo Giardinelli

Translation by Rhonda Dahl Buchanan

WHITE PINE PRESS | BUFFALO, NEW YORK

White Pine Press
P.O. Box 236
Buffalo, NY 14201
www.whitepine.org

Originally published by Editorial Edhasa, Ciudad Autónoma de Buenos
Aires as *La última felicidad de Bruno Fólner.*

Publication of this book was made possible, in part, with funds from the
University of Louisville, and under the auspices of work published within
the framework of the "SUR" Translation Support Program of the Ministry
of Foreign Affairs, International Trade and Worship of the Argentine Re-
public.

Translator's Acknowledgements:
I would like to thank the Programa Sur Translation Support Program and
the University of Louisville for their financial support. I would also like to
express my sincere appreciation to my first readers, who provided very useful
feedback for the manuscript: Robert Buchanan, Aída Batiste de la Fuente,
Mara Maldonado, and Susan and Nick Nicholson.

Printed and bound in the United States of America.

Cover photograph: Elaine LaMattina

ISBN: 978-1-945680-41-0

Library of Congress number: 2020930107

Bruno Fólner's Last Tango

"You're a grown man, that's to say washed-up, like all men your age, unless they're exceptional."

—Juan Carlos Onetti.
"Welcome, Bob"

1.

"Name?"

"Bruno Fólner," he said and immediately felt a dark satisfaction. He'd just invented himself.

The man gave him the keys to room 205, told him there was no elevator so he'd have to take the stairs, and that breakfast was served from seven to ten in the morning in the little bar overlooking the bay.

With one hand, he hung the briefcase over his shoulder. Inside was a laptop, passport, and $34,000. With the other hand, he picked up the carry-on bag and asked what time dinner was served, nodding his head when he heard beginning at eight and saying to himself, well Bruno, the dance has begun, though all he said out loud was a simple and polite "thanks." Then he climbed the stairs slowly, resolutely.

He was sixty-four years old, in good health, and although tired from the journey, he felt amazingly well. And it was no wonder: he'd finally made the second most important decision of his life. But this one was an old fantasy, which only in the last few months he'd planned and postponed for numerous reasons, each plausible, and they all came down to one: fear.

Perhaps things just take time, or maybe that old saying is true that man proposes and God disposes, etcetera, who knows, he said to himself as he climbed to the top floor. He wasn't exactly in a good mood, and yet he felt possessed by a kind of slight optimism that, oddly enough, filled him with guilt. A feeling that vanished as soon as he opened the door and with one look saw it was a lovely room. He was really going to like staying there.

The little inn was probably built ten to twelve years ago, in that distinctive contemporary Brazilian style, with large tiles and light colors, the large window, which at that hour of dusk offered a magnificent view of the sea, and everything he needed: a pine desk with a bleached wood finish and three drawers on one side, free Wi-Fi twenty-four hours a day, and a mini-bar he'd soon ask to be stocked to his desire. Against the wall, next to the bathroom was a double bed that seemed acceptable. His hands confirmed it had a good mattress, hard and firm. On the other wall, near the desk, was a sturdy pine wardrobe, simple and spacious, and inside, built into the wall, as he'd hoped, a safe in which he placed his documents and money.

Everything was fine to begin a new and final chapter of his life.

"The dance," he said looking at himself in the bathroom mirror, after approving the accommodations, and with a wide smile, as boyish and joyful as it was inappropriate. "Your last tango begins now, Bruno Fólner. What you did is done. No more blues."

And he returned to the bedroom, saw it was a little after seven, and giving in to exhaustion, he stretched out on the bed and stared at the ceiling fan as it turned slowly and quietly, perfectly, until he finally fell asleep.

2.

That same afternoon, when he arrived at the town, putting an end to his flight, just a few hours after having invented Bruno Fólner, even he didn't know that Praia Macacos could be a destination. He hadn't proposed it, had no plans or idea of where he'd wind up, although he did know, for some inexplicable but definitive reason, his escape would end in these parts. He knew if he continued to the north or northeast, he could make it to São Luis or Belém, which he'd read were very large cities, but he had no desire to hide out in that kind of metropolis. And further up, the continent came to an end. He'd looked at the map and studied the matter: beyond was Macapá and then the Guianas. He thought about continuing on, but suddenly came to the conclusion this was fine, that he didn't need to go any further, and besides, the region's tropical climate suited him and was good for the bronchial tubes of an ex-smoker and for his blood pressure, perpetually high and treacherous.

He arrived at the Pousada da Baleia, in Praia Macacos, by pure coincidence. Around noon that day, he simply boarded a coach bus that departed from the terminal in Fortaleza, with the intention of getting off wherever he felt like staying, and after traveling a little over an hour, it passed through there. The bus stopped at a small terminal painted bright red and orange, with a blue-tiled roof, which reminded him of the San Lorenzo Soccer Club, the colors of the Crows, he thought. And also Barcelona's. Still thinking about soccer, he got off to take a leak without letting go of the briefcase, then stretched his arms back to crack his vertebrae, and out of the corner of his eye, glimpsed the sea. From a small hill, he saw that the town, which spread out along the bay, was small, unpretentious, and charming. Out on the bay were some canoes and small light weight boats, the kind used by local fishermen, probably shrimpers, he imagined. He liked them, just as he liked the bay and the small size of the place, so he went back to the bus, checked to see if he'd forgotten anything, and got right off with the carry-on bag, never letting the briefcase out of his hand. He'd arrived. It didn't matter where. End of the road, he said to himself.

Soon afterwards, he learned the town was Praia Macacos and decided to stay there for the simple reason he liked the place. He asked about lodging, and was directed, halfway up the bay, to the Inn of the Whale, a little hotel that looked like of a family business, seemed clean, and couldn't have more than a dozen rooms. Above the front entrance, someone had painted a smiling blue whale, which he thought would bring him good luck. He was going to need it.

3.

It's me, he says, a while later as he looks at himself in the bathroom mirror. The very character who's being invented is me. My real name, the one that until now has been on my documents, doesn't matter. Or maybe it does, but I don't want to mention it. I've promised myself never to utter it out loud again. Let's just say the initials (phony, to be sure) were G. R. Well, G.R. has died. Not just Sarita. And I killed both of them.

He washes his face bent over the faucet, blows his nose, and after drying off, looks at his hands. Standing before the mirror, his reflection as still as a photograph, he observes the middle fingers of each hand. They're curling up, especially the one on the left, which already resembles a falcon claw. Sometimes, in the morning, his left hand feels like it's asleep. He shakes it and rubs his hands together until it feels normal again. So far his hands still function, but those freckles, those spots represent the relentless ticking of the clock.

He turns off the light and walks from the bathroom to the window and sees it's completely dark and thousands of flickering lights are dancing on the restless surface of the sea. For an instant, it seems everything in the world is bad, and a sudden panic comes over him that he dismisses, attributing it to exhaustion from the flights, layovers, and the long bus trip.

Everyone was informed this way: from the border, I sent an email to the kids, to my father-in-law Arturo, to Sarita's sister, and to my publishers, my agent, and a couple national news outlets and a few international ones that I know might take an interest. I also sent copies to two bookseller friends, to the only three colleagues I care about and whose opinions have always interested me, and to those friends of mine in the world who are like brothers: Alberto, who's a poet and teaches in Iowa, a guy as good as gold and the only one whose opinion truly matters to me; Lautaro, who lives and works in Tierra del Fuego studying marine algae and conducting experiments to find the perfect spirulina that can be mass-produced cheaply and save the world; and Elena, who began wandering all over Europe twenty years ago, and still hasn't stopped after half a dozen husbands and two kids she drags around like a Kolla Indian mother. None of her friends understand how she manages to stay so lovely and charming without money, and with the immigration police always hounding her.

To everyone he said more or less the same thing:

Subject: The passing of G.R. And in the text, so as not to cause them more unnecessary pain, or to be despised for some supposed depravation, he simply wrote:

"I'm leaving, disappearing; no one should look for me. I ended Sarita's life out of love and I hope you'll understand it that way, and if not, that's for each one of you to deal with. I'm not sick, I'm just leaving and I don't plan on returning. Forgive me if I hurt you, disappoint you, or anything like that, and I hope you'll forgive me if I leave behind any difficult unfinished business. I bear my own pain, and take all responsibility and blame for everything. Thank you for the love you gave me, and both of us. I've loved all of you nearly as much as Sarita loved you. Remember us fondly, if you can, and know that every time I think of you it will be with joy. A big hug to all of you, G."

And nothing more, he tells himself, stern and decisive. No excessive theatrics. Enough melodrama. Over.

His watch shows it just turned nine in the evening. Perfect time for dinner. He's hungry.

4.

Of course when it came to the kids it was harder. What adult hasn't thought some time, and more than once, about getting rid of his or her partner? I'm not saying you should go through with it, not even in your wildest dreams, but that fantasy about the disappearance of the other, male or female, does exist and can be consoling. Let's just say we dream, and not without pangs of guilt, that our partner disappears because of natural causes or an accident. That one day they take off, or get run over by a train, that they get sick and tired and clear out, mad as hell, or whatever. The fantasy of liberation is always enticing, above and beyond guilt. Refuse to admit it if you don't want to, don't accept it, but it's out there. And if on top of that there's an incurable cancer in the middle of it all, a progressive physical deterioration that starts with the annihilation of consciousness and condemns the patient from the get-go to a dreadful irreversible lethargy that doesn't kill instantly but wipes out any trace of humanity until there's nothing more of the victim than a thing that breathes artificially, you tell me if the desire isn't genuine for such a horror to end once and for all and for someone to tell you one bright morning that the person you loved has died and that life, your life, goes on.

5.

The phone on the night stand rings and it's Jorginho, the innkeeper. He asks him in Spanish, "*Senhor* Fólner, would you like to have dinner?"

He responds yes, that he was just about to come down, and while he slips into his loafers, without putting on socks, he thinks about the allure of that wonderful melodious language that is Portuguese, at least the Portuguese of Brazil. He pronounces the name of the inn out loud, A Pousada da Baleia, and thinks it sounds much nicer than La Posada de la Ballena. Then a wave of pleasure comes over him, after making yet another decision, this one only a minute ago: not to wear socks ever again in his life.

He looks at himself again in the bathroom mirror and combs in place the few hairs he has left. He smiles at that guy looking back at him, a rather forced smile, not fake but still forced. He's the same guy who last night saw his reflection in the little window of the bus and recognized himself. Or was that the night before? It doesn't matter, dismissing the thought with a shrug of his shoulders, as he walks over to the window that's open. He doesn't remember opening it, but doesn't give it a thought. He gazes at the sea, which looks fairly calm, with gentle waves that seem to ferry the lights of the town back and forth. No one's walking along the boardwalk. A white shadow can barely be seen about one hundred meters to the left, as if it were the ghost of a woman walking away barefoot, her hair blowing in the wind. Then a car passes by in the opposite direction, going way too fast. It all happens in a flash.

He leaves the room. Outside, in the hallway, there's nothing but an unexpected darkness, a minor concern no one else would question but reminds him of the night he fled.

He goes down the stairs concentrating like a chess master as he tries to focus on how comfortable his loafers feel, but unable to shake the memory of that last Sunday, before going to the hospital, when he mentioned at the table what he'd been thinking, without revealing he had a plan and would carry it out.

Marina didn't understand and got upset, very upset, sad at first, and then angry. What are you saying, what are you thinking about doing? Nothing, sweetheart, I'm just confused, don't pay attention to me.

There was no plan, to be honest, I didn't say anything like that. Only that perhaps — perhaps— we should consider the possibility of putting an end to *Mami*'s suffering.

It was a mistake, for sure. A mistake, then and now. He chastised himself, deeply annoyed that he had pronounced those words: "putting an end to *Mami*'s suffering," damn it, I didn't consider the impact of that phrase. I should have realized that obviously they'd take it the wrong way. At least Marina. How else would she have taken it? What an idiot I must be. A hurtful and careless slip-up for the daughter I loved. In fact, I'd mentioned the matter so that later her shock would be less painful, but everything ended terribly.

As for Nico, he didn't say a word and got up, grim. And Tomi said he planned to spend the night at the hospital on Monday after coming back from the university, then went over to the computer to distract himself. Not one of them understood his need to talk, not one wanted to even hear him out, listen to the mere idea, the possibility, the proposition. It didn't interest them, even as a fantasy to buy time for his lack of courage.

Of course it was understandable, but that didn't keep him from feeling a bit angry because they, he said to himself, couldn't understand my frame of mind. At their age, there's a total lack of respect for certain ideas and decisions made by adults. And I don't blame them, they just couldn't understand it. They must have thought it was one of those crazy ideas of the old man and maybe they were right. But the frustration created an abyss: if they couldn't understand my hesitation, and weren't willing to even talk about the matter, they certainly wouldn't accept any action I might take. It was absurd for me to think they could put themselves in my shoes.

He chooses a table near the largest window that overlooks the sea, unreservedly, like a mother-in-law. He orders a bottle of Trapiche Sauvignon Blanc, which arrives submerged in a bucket of ice, and asks for the menu, *la carta, por favor.*

6.

While he decides, he smiles to himself, thinking that in fact it was a matter of *cartas*, letters. He wrote each one of them a handwritten letter, which he mailed at the post office at the last hour of the last afternoon. It was very brief. I'm leaving, he said, I can't stand to see *Mami*, the woman all four of us love, suffer any longer, and that's why I prefer to end it, for her and for me. It was going to end someday anyway, and the sooner the better. I have no courage to do it; just an unbearable exhaustion that I'd never know how to explain to you, nor would you understand.

Then he thanked them for their love and encouraged them to remain close to each other. We were a lovely family until destiny, or whatever you want to call it, ruined the party, he wrote, crossed out, then wrote again. But every party comes to an end and I'd like this one to end without reproach. In the postscript, he assured them they'd be financially secure and lack nothing. He'd left a power of attorney with the Perotti Clerk's Office in all three of their names, and sent another to his agency in Barcelona, arranging an equal distribution, now and in the future, of his royalties. It wasn't a lot, but it was what it was. "Have compassion for me," he said at the end, "and don't blame me too much, after all, this will be a relief for all of you too. And don't look for me, don't pull a 'Grand Teresita.' Kisses and love always and thank you once again, *Papá*."

Yes, that had been the hardest thing. It still is, he says to himself as he settles into the chair and removes the cap from the fountain pen he always carries in the pocket of his shirts. It's an old Parker 51 that he treasures, a gift from Sarita when he turned fifty-one years old. He writes: Let me tell you now, as a necessary digression, that Teresita is the name of my sister-in-law, an intelligent, hard-working woman, full of energy and high moral standards, but whose husband, Sarita's brother, Uncle Lucas, abandoned at the end of the nineties because he was up to his eyeballs in debt. Or maybe he didn't love her anymore, and one day felt defeated, but at the same time so fed up he was ready for a bold move. Whatever it was, is not my business. What is certain is that Lucas took off, and for many months, much more than a year, he wandered from province to province, until he landed in Patagonia, in a fishermen village between Comodoro and Caleta Oliva, in northern Santa Cruz. He set up a kiosk that turned into a general store and worked really hard and began to prosper. Until one day Teresita arrived, after moving heaven and earth, as they say, to find him. She reported him missing to police stations and courts all over the country, plastered fliers in cities and towns with Lucas's photo, contracted private detectives, and searched herself, with map in hand and the tenacity of an ant, for the possible whereabouts of her vanished husband. Until following improbable tracks and clues, she arrived in that shitty village one Sunday in November, a cold and blustery afternoon, and as if sniffing his trail, she came to that inlet where he was sitting on the dock, with his feet dangling, as he calmly and idly wiggled the bait and float.

"Hello Lucas, I found you," she said to him casually, without making a scene, and Lucas heard that voice and turned around, as meekly as an old bull, and responded with feigned tenderness, "Hi Tere, it's been a while," and no one in the world could have said for certain if it was a smile or panic that crossed his face.

Teresita gestured for him to keep fishing, if that's what he was doing, and sat down next to him and began to prepare the *mate*, taking it out of the bag that also held a thermos of hot water. She brewed one and handed it to him as if only a few minutes had passed since the last, and not two years. And they're still living there, in that same village, as tranquil and undisturbed as the two of them, together perhaps only because they had the good sense, or wisdom, not to make a single reproach.

I love my brother and sister-in-law, he thinks, nodding his head to no one, just as I loved my mother and father-in-law. I told them in another email, "Forgive me for the pain I've caused you, but I swear to you Sarita's resting in peace now. Forgive me, please, because the death of a sister, like that of a daughter, is an irreversible act, but I'm absolutely convinced I did the right thing. That's why, wherever I am, I'm going to imagine the loving indulgence of both of you. The kids are provided for, and I believe the two of you will suffer less as well. Don't look for me, don't wait for me. I'm not coming back."

7.

The crab, served fresh from the sea and covered with melted parmesan, was impeccable. Although crabs are also plentiful in the Chaco, supposedly just as heavy and meaty, when they come out of the Río Negro, they seem to have lost their reddish tinge and look dirty, speckled, and sometimes battered. Must be the polluted water, he thinks, but back there no one would eat a crab. And yet here, they're delicious.

Two glasses of wine helped to wash them down splendidly. Later perhaps a crème brûlée and chamomile tea. And after dinner, a Cointreau. All the while contemplating the calm sea under that immense night sky.

He tells Jorginho and his wife, Dona Amalia, that he's never tasted anything so scrumptious, and they smile with pride, as does Caio, the kid who works as cook and dishwasher. He's black and his eyes are light-colored, not exactly blue, but like crystal clear water. He has very curly hair, who knows if natural, or from a salon, with tubular ringlets, nothing like those thick Rastafarian dreadlocks. Dona Amalia calls him Caími, with affection, when she asks him in the evenings to play her a few *choros* on his guitar, traditional melodies that, as a Carioca, fill her with nostalgia for her native Río de Janeiro.

They're all so nice that an entire life with them would be insufferable, thinks Bruno Fólner, who suddenly feels like a lucky man. Although he immediately chides himself for being so foolish, what luck, he corrects himself, what the hell am I talking about, or rather, thinking, what luck if I just came from assassinating my wife?

Yes, that's what I did, don't play dumb, Fólner, assassination is killing someone with premeditation and malice. Technically, that was what you did, perhaps without malice but premeditated, most definitely premeditated.

"Yes of course, *gosto muito*," he responds to Jorginho's inquiry. He doesn't know what the question was, but he responded politely, yes, a courteous and preemptive yes. Jorginho smiles and serves him another helping of crab that he brings quickly from the kitchen, as if he'd had it ready, moving as swiftly as a colt breaking out of the gate, while Bruno remembers he once did taste something equally delicious. It was during a long weekend he spent with Danila, some fifteen years ago, or a century and a half, he doesn't know. Danila, also a Carioca, had eyes as green as her flag, what a beautiful woman, at least in his memory, she seems more beautiful now than she probably was. She spoke with that same lilting music on her lips, in her voice, like a samba, and she enjoyed making love, moaning and panting, and as she climaxed, she'd burst out laughing, and keep laughing for a while, content as a happy little girl. Then she'd fall asleep and he'd look at her, just as gratified. Her body was magnificent, slender and lanky, finished off by strong and shapely legs, and tiny feet, which she flaunted, showing off her brightly painted toes in flip-flops or wedged sandals, with high cork heels, and leather or straw straps. She was a lovely example of a girl from Ipanema, tall with ample hips, and even more lovely remembering her now, feeling the soft sea breeze passing through the open picture windows.

Gazing at the night, not letting the swaying of the white curtains distract him, he wondered why he happened to remember Danila at that very moment, seeing her so clearly and so happy in those bygone days. Because of guilt, of course, which ruins everything. But we men are geniuses when it comes to self-indulgence. Just as Sarita was with her intuition, her relentless and agonizing suspicion. Of course he denied everything, calling her crazy, delusional, and other choice adjectives, until that one weekend after getting it on with Danila, all hell broke loose at home. And if everything didn't go to hell it was because of Sarita, whose decision to forget the affair turned out to be a supreme gesture of generosity. Macho to the end, you came out ahead, you asshole, he says to himself now. Well, he counters quickly, but that guy was someone else, G.R., the one who later murdered Sarita, not this one. And he takes a break from his thoughts to swallow another mouthful of crab that doesn't taste quite as exquisite. He washes it down with a swig of wine, smacks his lips, and adds a couple ice cubes to his glass. And what do you think about that, Fólner? That I'm another person. That's right.

And now he can't help but think there are lovely memories that become even more beautiful if you honor them, if you reward them with a third serving of crab with parmesan, like the one he's savoring now, accompanied by a green salad and a few sips of Sauvignon Blanc. *Tudo bem.*

And to top it off, I'll have a little dessert to celebrate, a few slices of pineapple with a scoop of vanilla ice cream, what more could I want?

He smiles at no one in particular and nods his head, muttering, yes, I once was an adulterer.

Just then he sees an illuminated boat pass by and tells himself that one day he should go out on the bay. Then he accepts the mug Dona Amalia brings him, and as he idly stirs a cube of sugar in the coffee, his thoughts return to Danila, and that reminiscence turns out to be the perfect image to crown that inaugural dinner of welcome he's given himself, he thinks, because that night marks the birth of Bruno Fólner.

Congratulations, Bruno. Welcome, Bruno, he thinks and whispers as he empties the glass of ice cold wine. Then he drinks the coffee and asks for the bill, signs it, and walks over to the stairs to go up to his room. Yes, give me a wake-up call at nine, thank you. I'm so tired, I'll fall asleep right away, he says to himself. Like a baby boy who's sixty some years old.

8.

He'd remembered a few moments from their honeymoon in Hawaii, as if they were engraved on the glass of the bus window. They were like cubes drawn by an imaginary Picasso over the transparent surface that looked out on the night, shifting cubes that composed the painting of his memories. He seemed to recognize fragments of happy moments that fell into place slowly, like pieces of a puzzle, of the two of them on the beach, hugging each other and smiling with the hotel in the background, a photo Sarita adored. A strange and spontaneous flicker of lights blurred the embrace slightly and accentuated the sparkle in their eyes.

Leaning over the railing of a balcony of the hotel, in the upper right-hand corner of the photo, another couple is embracing each other, as if two lenses had captured joy reproduced several times over. Bruno remembered that moment, and with a blink recalled another photo someone took of them on a street corner in downtown San Francisco: this one was of a staged kiss we gave each other standing next to a smiling red-headed police officer, during a layover of nearly fifteen hours that we took advantage of to see the sights. He never knew who actually took that photo of them, but for certain it was taken the day before the first night in Hawaii, when Nico was conceived, or at least Sarita was always convinced of that.

That glass, which peered out on the night and the invisible pampas and seemed to move in the wind, resembled a tarnished mirror that reflected the faces of Tomi and Marina, next to Nico. He saw the three of them singing, laughing at some party, at some Sunday family meal, or perhaps the celebration for Sarita, when she turned forty-three, just two weeks before she got sick the first time.

Life's not a bitch, he thinks when he gets to his room, or it doesn't have to be, even though it can screw you, as it just did. Not Sarita's actual death, he's quick to correct himself, but that it wiped out her happy and carefree existence, condemning her to be tethered to a breathing machine. And converting her husband into a criminal.

9.

Fólner, of course, is the simple phonetic pronunciation in Spanish of Faulkner. My favorite writer, the great Bill Faulkner. A master who isn't read much these days, a shame, but oh well, fuck those idiots who read popular books, best sellers promoted by the market, well-edited and even better publicized, but fluff in ninety-nine percent of the cases. He remembers the characters Baricco describes in his *"I Barbari,"* that brilliant book he read a while ago, and says to himself, so much for those morons and their mentors, those fanatic barbarians of Hollywood pop culture. And he also recalls a Barrico novel he didn't like so much. Better Faulkner, he says to the darkness. You can't have it all.

To fall asleep, he watches the fan spin round. The paddles create a kind of film in black and white on the ceiling whose plot is incomprehensible, but without a doubt, interesting. Every so often a car drives down the boardwalk and the glare ricocheting from the headlights alters the patterns, like shifting black and gray designs in a kaleidoscope that are never the same.

He wonders about Sarita, what could have happened to her body, who must have found her dead. But he immediately abandons all hope for an answer, dismissing such black thoughts by shaking his head side to side as if spinning them away, thinking, I don't want to enter the dark jungle.

He feels his heart pounding. It's not tachycardia, but only that he's concentrating on the silence of the room and the night. Silence is just a saying, because the sound of the sea can be heard, the endless chatter of that gigantic blowhard who never shuts up and at times roars in fury. He closes his eyes and conjures his own image reflected on the glass wall of the airport in Foz, minutes before boarding the plane. He was wearing a very classy brown jacket made of *carpincho* leather, and beneath it a khaki shirt, like that of a hunter or union worker, and slightly faded jeans, and Oggi loafers in a matching brown shade, a bit lackluster from so much walking. He could easily pass for who he was, a man in his sixties, still active and engaged. Indeed a benevolent glance would have sized him up as an intriguing man in his fifties, although somewhat worn-out.

That tall guy, a bit flushed, gray haired and balding, with the neck of a bull and wide shoulders was him, when he went by another name, the name he had all his life. And that only yesterday, or the day before, he decided to kill, and he did kill him. He did away with his name like someone who ends a life. Bruno Fólner did it.

He's distracted for a few seconds by the sound of the waves, growing louder the more the sea breeze blows. He gets up and closes the window, and for an instant thinks that he never opened it, once again not remembering having opened it, but what does it matter. And when he returns to the bed and back to his memories, he admits something he can't deny, that in the exact space, which had been occupied hours before by a homicidal decision that went far beyond any justification, there is now a lot of anxiety and some fear.

He says to the shadows that he needs to stop, turn off the engine. After managing to get this far, I'm fine, he thinks and murmurs. I'm okay. Everything's fine. I'm someone who's arrived at a destination, at a destiny like any other, nothing special, and he knows it but can't calm down. I see it clearly and that's all there is to it. I was about to change my mind, and I believe I went through with it out of true love for Sarita and so I wouldn't have to see myself as such a coward. Faulkner, the real one, would've despised me. He'd have pegged me to be another Francis Macomber confronting a lion, although that guy was one of Hemingway's characters.

There are many remedies for insomnia, all useless. Bruno Fólner looks at the ceiling and the turning paddles that mark the slow tempo of the passing minutes. He counts each turn until he loses count. He says to himself that he should read something, but it's a fleeting thought, unconvincing. He notices a slight feeling of suffocation, a minor difficulty in breathing that seems to occur because of a sudden cardiac arrhythmia. No, he doesn't believe his blood pressure has risen, but he recognizes the fear that overcomes him each time he feels that compression in his chest and he can't get enough air. He thinks and fears the same thing: that without realizing it, he could be entering the eternal dream. I'll find out soon enough, he says to himself.

I don't know how to be suicidal or homicidal, he argues, because I don't feel fear, desperation, or hate. The one who surely felt all that was Lugones. That's not my case.

He closes his eyes and thinks about Sarita and her final blind gaze, a blank stare. There was no fear in them, no reproach, no guilt; there was nothing in those eyes he'd loved so much, only emptiness.

Sarita was dead when I killed her.

He slowly begins to dream that many hands are throwing stones at him from the opposite sidewalk.

IO.

Like in the movies and soaps, a new scene begins with the ringing of the telephone.

"*Bon dia, Senhor* Fólner," says Jorginho in his language, adding, "it's nine o'clock and a beautiful morning."

"*Obrigado,*" he responds and puts down the phone. He gets up, goes to the bathroom, takes an eternal piss, and gets dressed for a day on the beach: shorts, t-shirt, flip-flops. He plans to go for a swim after eating breakfast and writing a bit.

He slept little, although very deeply and feels rested, but on that clear morning beaming with sunshine, something's troubling him. He decides at that very moment that when he goes downstairs, he'll take a look at the Argentine newspapers before breakfast, especially those from the Chaco; he'll also check out the usual two or three second-rate websites and sniff around to see what's going on there, what's happening on the reservation, as he likes to call the local gossip mill.

But someone's using the public computer and he left his Mac in the room, so he serves himself some scrambled eggs, juice, and coffee, and finds a spot far from the big window with a view of the sea. Guests are having breakfast at several tables and he senses that he's nervous and on edge. He feels as if an incisive and inescapable gaze is present, scrutinizing and cornering him. Those dead eyes he's dreamed about suddenly open and come back to life, luminous, inquisitive, beautiful as in those years when they lived in El Paso, before the kids came along. Not the gringo El Paso, he always had to clarify, but the one in the province of Corrientes. How presumptuous those folks from Corrientes were naming the towns Paso de los Libres on the coast of the Uruguay River and Paso de la Patria on the Paraná River. The latter is a charming little town, friendly and tranquil, lined with beaches and sandbars that seem like the Caribbean.

In that house, he recalls, as he sips a delicious glass of mango juice, there was a pair of owls who'd always stare at us with the same intense curiosity as those lively eyes of Sarita. With that same piercing scrutiny. We called them The Gazers because they'd gaze at us all day long, in the fork of a tree, on the most horizontal branch of the tallest pine tree in the garden; actually it was more of a park than a garden, with those magnificent rows of mango and guava trees, flamboyan and *mamón* trees. We never knew exactly where they made their nest because we always saw them in the crook of the pine tree, keeping each other silent company in the strangest but most intriguing way. Perhaps they lived further up, or who knows where, but they'd spend all their time, every day, on that branch, perched next to each other, gazing at us with their enormous round eyes, or looking at each other, cuddling together at times, grooming each other. The Gazers were precious company in those days, because when I first settled down in El Paso, I was a single guy who spent all his time writing, and every once in a while, a woman would spend the night, until I met Sarita and asked her to live with me, and in less than a month, she made herself right at home, and from El Paso she continued her studies until she got her degree. For both of us, the Gazers were phenomenal companions. And when we had to leave the town after that incredible flood and move to the city, no longer seeing them, abandoning them, was one of the deepest losses. We never saw them again, nor were we ever watched by them, which was the most important thing, and of course I couldn't imagine what they must have done without us. We had become a family, almost. And all families fall apart at some point; that's a fact.

Dona Amalia replenishes the cold cuts and cheeses on the long and laden buffet, where guests can serve themselves, and meanwhile, signals with her finger and a smile that the computer in the lobby is available.

In a few minutes of surfing the net, he catches up on what everyone knows and confirms that no one's after him. At least no one has filed a report, neither the police nor the doctors, and Sarita's death isn't newsworthy.

But also in their online versions, the local press doesn't include obituaries. He'd have to check the printed newspapers, but that's impossible there. He recalls a story he read years ago: a guy goes to the town cemetery one night and digs up the body of his mother and places it in the tomb of his father, who had died forty years before. So as to unite their idealized love for eternity, he places them as if they were gazing at each other, pelvis to pelvis, and he covers them with dirt. Death is not only inescapable; it's also infinite in the rituals it inspires.

End of story: he closes the search engine. Time to move on.

II.

He walks for a while in silence as he weighs the consequences of his decision to stay there. It was a long and cautious journey that brought him to this town, he says to himself, with ambiguous approval, while somewhat pleasant thoughts are disturbed by recurring feelings of guilt and reproach. It's true he had to kill Sarita. It was just three days ago that he disconnected her in the early hours of dawn. And he has no regrets. He knows or believes he knows that he shouldn't feel guilty but rather relieved, and even what some experts would call "satisfaction for having fulfilled a duty." But no.

Of course you never know.

But he's not that afraid either, although he senses a little fear. Fate can be a good ally in certain circumstances, for example, when you run away at night. And he landed in this little town by pure chance, so there's no reason, evidence, or circumstance that would lead them to come looking for me here, he says to himself, no one would think about coming to this little seaside town to ask questions. Ninety-nine to one.

Of course you never know.

He loves the houses painted bright colors, those blues, reds, greens, and yellows that seem to chatter, like parrots, about the lives of their inhabitants. A hill rises above that small town, not so high but enough to offer a view of the hustle and bustle that takes place in the morning, or at dusk, a slightly deceptive one because during the long hours of the day, the heat only encourages endless siestas, laziness, or sin.

It's also true there are two or three photos of him on the internet, taken recently, but he's not famous. Outside his country, and if he stays away from certain places, he won't run serious risks, although he should take precautions and always, as much as possible, lie low. Praia Macacos, on the northern coast of Brazil, seems just the perfect place. It's a very small town at the tip of a bay, like a thousand others all along the Atlantic coast. It has no luxury hotel, it's not a developed tourist destination, and has no big shopping centers or night life. Argentines would never invade those beaches.

Two painful nights brought him there, perhaps the worst of his life, especially the first, which will remain seared in his memory forever. For sure. No other night was as arduous, no other required such concentration and painstaking attention to detail, and in some way, none was as risky.

Without a doubt, the night you kill your wife has to be devastating.

But I'm okay now, he repeats to himself, I feel fine.

Not in the least uneasy, or troubled.

12.

As the sun sets over the continent, and shadows gradually blanket the sea, which he gazes at every so often through the window, he writes on a napkin: "The reason for his discretion was as simple as this: he needed to hide out for a long time, in other words, just as he too was planning now, to make himself vanish for whatever time was left to live. He had killed his wife and had no intention of going to jail, and that was that." Period.

He folds the paper and wonders where he put his notebook. It must be in the room, on the desk. Then he unfolds the napkin again so he can write something else.

The only thing that comes to mind is an old saying from a book he can't remember: "Death is a certainty that can only be questioned in dreams."

He stands to go upstairs and look for his red Moleskine. Because Bruno Fólner also writes by hand and with a ballpoint pen or with the Parker, in his red Moleskine. For him, the need to write is frustrating, an urgency that tends to show up like a ghost exerting a compulsive demand. But he sits down again and unfolds the napkin without writing a single word and admits he's confused, where the hell could I have left it, as if searching for it in the air to no avail, while scolding himself: I must have it with me always, like a hunter on the prowl, there's no turning back for a writer, leaving only a word or two scratched out here and there, on lines previously written, traces of his trail. He loves the romantic notion of crossing out words and writing others above, lines that at times illuminate and clarify as they snake along the margins and around the edges. And then later, but only later, comes the time to transfer the drafts to the computer. Nowadays that seems unnatural because writing by hand is a lost art, but the notebook should come first. For me, outlines, notes, ideas, first go into a ledger book with oilcloth covers, they say that Isidoro Blaisten used to say. And before him, Juan Filloy and before him hundreds, thousands, millions, all the poets and writers the world has ever known.

He stands to go upstairs to look for it in his room. Because Bruno Fólner also writes by hand in a red Moleskine, hell, he says smiling into the twilight and noticing out of the corner of his eye a small white cruise ship entering the bay from the south. It will make its way north, slowly and surely, glowing like a dazzling bride.

He goes upstairs, gets the red notebook and comes back down, then sits and looks at the sea like someone gazing back in time. That cruise ship reminds him of his own unfulfilled dream to be a sailor, remembering, that was the wish of my old man who arrived at Puerto Barranqueras in the 1930s, during the decline of the corrupt government of Justo the Unjust, as he used to call that general who became president in 1932 by buying votes. Tough times. *Papá* arrived by steamboat, on the *Berlín*, which had two enormous paddlewheels, on the port and starboard sides, and passed by Corrientes, six times a month, up the river, or on its way down from Asunción.

Now, many years later and very far from there, Bruno Fólner stares at the Atlantic as if searching in that boat for something that's not on the sea but in his memory. The *Nicolás Ambrosoni* was also a white cruise ship, a riverboat that was just as small. A little boat that weighed seventy tons and sailed the river beginning in 1913. They say it was the first boat with a diesel motor to sail on the Paraná River. And that must have been true because its noisy engine deafened the nearly eighty passengers it carried, the majority of them students who packed it several times a day, every day, going between Chaco and Corrientes. That's where he met Sarita, who was just beginning her degree in Biology, and was like a Hebrew sun over the river, a splendid beauty who made him fall in love in an instant and forever.

There were three or four years of weekly crossings, studying on board, playing cards, and chatting with classmates and professors on that trip that lasted a little over an hour. Construction of the long bridge that joins the two provinces hadn't been finished yet, and we all knew we were witnesses to the end of an era. The rocking when the river was choppy, the cold or heat on board, the chatter and terrible coffee they served at the bar on the stern, all was going to be forgotten with the inauguration of the bridge.

Once in Buenos Aires, years later, on an inlet of the Tigre, he discovered the *Nicolás Ambrosoni* keeled over on its side, damaged, filthy and abandoned, and he thought about buying it, having it fixed up and painted in a good shipyard. He checked out the costs, looked into what it would take to get it up and running, and when he returned home, Sarita laughed at first, and then, when she realized he was serious, she told him he was out of his mind and swore that if he followed through with the crazy idea, he'd have to choose between her or that useless heap of junk.

With the Parker lying exhausted in his hand and tears in his eyes, Bruno Fólner sighs, devastated at the realization that he'll never again see that beloved ship sailing, nor on the rail, waving at him with intense melancholy, the ghost of Sarita. He bites his lips and suddenly notices that the night will be a party, like every night, beautiful with a calm sea, deep and dark blue, and the perfect breeze. On the other hand, all of a sudden, he realizes everything inside him is eternal sorrow because he doesn't know what he's done, if it was an atrocity or the act of mercy he wants to believe it was, that he desperately needs to believe. Sometimes the women of the coast are so beautiful that to take them down a peg, we allow ourselves to become overwhelmed by dark thoughts, just the opposite of such beauty, perhaps to compensate for things because we can't handle such perfection.

Our love story was one-of-a-kind, he tells himself, because Sarita was one-of-a-kind.

He's embarrassed that he's only capable of trite clichés, while the pain surges like a tsunami, and he suddenly feels his face contorting like a childish pout, and he bursts into tears.

13.

On that splendid morning, the third or fourth day, which one doesn't matter to him, Bruno Fólner leaves the inn and heads left, toward the hill about a kilometer to the north. The sea flaunts its perpetual beauty, the sky is bright blue, and he feels well, limber and full of energy. He can't remember if he had a dream, and that lapse in his memory suits him just fine.

He hesitated at first, on his way out, when a feeling of sudden cowardice came over him, but then convinced himself he had no choice, that sooner or later the whole town would know he was there. If they didn't know already about him, the outsider, in such a small town. So he climbs the stairs to the boardwalk, two at a time, like a much younger guy and ventures forth — smiling as he thinks about using that verb, at his age — determined to take a walk on that perfect morning.

Then he sees her. The woman in the long white dress he'd caught a glimpse of a few nights ago, somewhat surreal but clear, as she is now, wandering down the boardwalk.

He keeps her in sight: there's something about her fleeting figure that attracts him. An inexplicable magnetism. Though she's not exactly a beautiful woman, her allure is, one could say, bountiful, an appeal that exudes an unusual harmony. Off in the distance, the woman stops and faces the waves, statuesque, like a sentry on a watchtower. Still and focused, she simply gazes at the horizon, as if her eyes could encompass all that vast surface.

Bruno Fólner walks slowly toward her, as if distracted, feigning an innocent curiosity for some point on the horizon. When he comes within ten meters or so, he pretends to be interested in something particular, and stops at a position parallel to her, at just the right angle, about forty-five degrees, so if someone were to trace imaginary straight lines, their eyes could make contact at a not so distant point. That tactic allows him to observe her with a certain pretense. Or so he believes.

But he's able to watch her out of the corner of his eye and admire her dark beauty. Her thick black hair falls down her back and covers her face, whenever the sea breeze blows a certain way. A typical Brazilian beauty, says Bruno Fólner to himself, as he boldly scrutinizes the appearance of the woman. Small, straight nose, very black eyebrows, plump lips. Her slender neck resembles the root of a tree branching out on either side and ending in a pair of perfect brown shoulders glistening in the sun, from which a pair of ample breasts are suspended, firm, buoyant and round. It's obvious she wears no bra, which makes her even more attractive. Her body is that of a woman who gave birth years ago, and that maternity is apparent in her large pointy nipples, as desirable as lips, and in the slight thickness of her waist. Her wide and sturdy feet peek out beneath the strapless white dress, which flows like a long tunic to her ankles.

Bruno Fólner imagines that woman must make love with deeply sensual and passionate surrender. He smiles as he ponders that thought, and gives in to the nostalgia of imagining how beautiful it would've been to love such a woman twenty years ago. She must be absolutely perfect lying naked in bed, as sublime as the beautiful and determined ease with which he imagines she reaches her orgasms, moaning as if singing, how marvelous. He says to himself: how marvelous, and immediately wonders why he's so obsessed with erotic fantasies, an old guy, Bruno, stop fucking around, he berates himself without mercy. A guy who's past his prime, true, but still full of desire to screw, he counters, suddenly annoyed. Maybe not as red-hot as in younger days, but with expertise or whatever it takes, my desire is intact, what the hell. Frustrated but intact.

Penetrating her must be like swinging in a park at dusk, without witnesses, or the clamor of the city.

Then he says to himself, what bullshit, and starts walking again toward the piers below the small hill on which the town seems to slumber in its tropical dream. When he passes behind the woman, she doesn't even move. Naturally, he says to himself, and keeps on going.

14.

The truth is I wanted to leave. I'd been thinking about it for some time. Sarita and I had loved each other very much and for a long time, but in those last years everything had turned cold, or to be more exact, routine. Watching the kids grow up, as great as that can be when it's great, also leads to emptiness and restlessness. Many times, I found myself bored, and presumably she was too, although we never talked about that. If we had, I don't know if we could've stood being together.

But who knows. Sometimes speaking about boredom clears the air. Or it condemns you to something worse.

But what happened was what happened: first the stroke, the blood clot that made her brain stop functioning, and then came the tests, CAT scans, and the final diagnosis of an incurable, irreversible case. I wasn't prepared for that, I suppose no one is. But I knew immediately that I was not willing to be an impassive witness to that tragedy, and that there was no reason for Sara to suffer that shitty deterioration. No one in the world, no reason or right can force you to endure that supposed survival, which relies on electrodes and tubes that provide anything but life.

I realized that one early morning, the hour when silence vanquishes the night, and in the hospital everything slows to a halt, down to the most minimal thing, and the drip of a faucet in the bathroom can be heard and lull you to sleep. It's an instant in which time seems to stop, as if pleasures, or the possibility of pleasure, are wiped out completely and forever, and one knows, like Truman Capote's death row convict, that the new day will bring no hope.

15.

After drinking two cups of coffee, he wipes his mouth with a napkin, stands up and looks at the sea, sensing a kind of desire as he gazes at it. He remembers Danila in Niteroi, wading into the sea and parting the waves with her hands with the serious concentration of a tailor. Back then, he wasn't burdened with resentment and simply gave himself permission to enjoy himself as he wished. The world seemed wide enough that Sarita could be back home on the landlocked reservation enjoying her tidy and peaceful life, while he could be at the seashore delighting in that woman with those magnificent breasts.

What an asshole I've been, he says to himself without feeling even a tinge of guilt. Male, said the midwife, when G.R. was born.

You're no different, Bruno Fólner. You were born from the same womb.

He greets Jorginho, who asks him if he needs anything.

"*Não, obrigado, tudo bem,*" he says, adding, "just some help from the god of the sea to write."

And he sits down at the little table that looks out on the boardwalk.

16.

It's true, I wanted to leave, and that was my opportunity. I felt like a bastard, if you must know, but I also told myself it was my last card and if I didn't play it, I was going to lose anyway, he thinks as he looks at the sea and watches a fairly swanky yacht, about fifteen meters long, passing by.

"It's not from here," he murmurs, while observing some people on deck. They seem to look at him, but he knows that's not the case. They're tourists checking out Praia Macacos. They'll take a few photos, maybe anchor at the dock to refresh the beer and ice supply, and head on their merry way.

"And I played it," he muttered softly, barely moving his lips. Sarita had no other future and neither did I. After doing it, the only thing left was for me to go away physically, and Brazil, Mexico, or a remote island in the Caribbean were my three favorite and oldest fantasies. And since, in fact, it came down to an escape, what better than fleeing to literature, which is never a bad destiny, and I owed it to myself. For at least two years, I'd been fantasizing about a novel that had never gotten off the ground. And for even longer, I'd begun to see myself for who I really was: a washed up, empty-headed writer, turned mediocre for who knows how many repeated failures, real or imaginary.

I was mortified, just as I am now, by my own literary silence over the past decade. And also the apathy, lack of solidarity, and rampant brutality in the country distracted me to the point of exasperation. It was hard for me to recognize it, and I never would've admitted it, but I felt very bitter professionally, and about all I could do was muster up plans to run away to who knows where, hypothetical idiotic escapes. I hated the journalists who couldn't conceal their envy for those they interviewed, and the critics who praised to the hilt mediocre writers with some renown, believing that those second-rate celebrities could deliver them from anonymity. I despised those professors who blatantly overlooked authors, important living and dead writers, and then published articles that no one read about the same two or three names that they themselves canonized. In the professional circles of the man now called Bruno Fólner, the game consisted of plagiarizing and giving the same speech a thousand times, incorporating whatever trendy buzz words or expressions were in style, and repeating them like maniacs. I was fed up with all that and with my own classes at the university, although I was reluctant to recognize it: fed up with seeing myself talking like an idiot to dozens of students who only wanted to mess around the way adolescents mess around, or to screw like cats, while I asked myself what the hell was I doing there, hating them because they were my perfect excuse for not writing. And in fact they were, the students and that whole scene: a perfect excuse, a reason for paralysis and resentment.

"I played the card," he repeats to himself, as if to clear away once and for all the doubts and guilt that held him back and kept him from creating one fucking sentence that was worthwhile. "But I'll never know if I did the right thing."

He gets up feeling frustrated once again, and sees there's no sign of that yacht in the bay, and then goes up to his room and lies down on the bed. Sick and tired of being fed up.

First he gazed at her intensely for a very long time. Certainly more than an hour, lost in the looming silence of the hospital. He contemplated her gaunt features as if looking at a dead bird on a sandy beach. He focused on her tightly drawn lips, which he had loved so much in other times, and traced his fingers over her barely visible eyebrows and the eyelids that would never again allow anyone to see the splendor of her blue eyes, once sparkling and transparent as aquamarine gems. At no moment did he cry or allow his emotions to get the best of him. The decision was sealed after the final conversation with Farruggi, who in all honesty had told him there was nothing more the doctors could do except keep her alive artificially — those were his words — for as long as her body held out; medicine has limits that aren't always reached because it's not an exact science, but the statistics are conclusive in cases like this one, and I can't offer you even a one percent probability of recovery. After saying that, he patted him on the shoulder in a manner that to him, whose name was not yet Bruno Fólner, seemed more a gesture of condolence than anything else.

And it also seemed to him that he'd spent an eternity at Sarita's side in those long early morning hours of February 14th, staring at her in silence with the coldness of a polar bear that he didn't recognize in himself.

Today he doesn't know, he can't remember, at what exact minute he got up the courage and did it.

It was hard to kill Sarita, but merciful.

An act of love, Bruno Fólner tells himself now.

I don't know if you must have cold blood, but certainly balls, to finish off the woman you loved for so many years. A young woman, beautiful, as luminous as a two-hundred watt lightbulb and as ardent as a burning log of pine. In any case, you have to have balls, and cold blood. He'd never killed anyone before, but in the instant he made the decision, he knew there was no turning back.

During the previous twenty-four hours, he'd planned every step. And in the early hours of that day, he didn't hesitate: he disconnected everything as soon as the night nurse made her rounds. First he adjusted Sarita's head on the pillow and removed the saline drip from the vein in her arm, the respirator from her mouth, the other shitty little tube inserted into an artery on the right side of her neck, and then he stood there looking at her for a long while. As tears filled his eyes from the growing pain and guilt he was suffering, he very delicately pried open Sarita's eyes with two fingers to see if there was any light in them, any life, but there was nothing more than a blank mist, a vast emptiness. Those eyes, which he'd loved, didn't show any vital signs and their listless glassy appearance was one piece of evidence of the agony of the throes of death: she'd been dying slowly like a fish in the sun that opens and closes its gills until it remains lifeless.

At one point, he thought that if she had made a conscious effort to open her eyes, she'd have looked at him with gratitude. She'd have appreciated the act, even, which was nothing more than the resolution of an unspoken pact of love. An unexpected resolution, what's more, because Sarita was twenty years younger than him and that irreversible cancer had been a God-awful twist of fate. She'd never again wake up, or open her eyes, or move a muscle. That's what Faruggi and Ramos Cordera had declared with their omissions and convoluted way of speaking, and it was evident. All they could do was stick damn tubes everywhere, even up her ass, to top it all off.

Obviously he wasn't an assassin, but to whom was he going to explain this. Life itself was the assassin, and he wasn't going to go to jail for that killer, not even for one day. He refused to subject himself to stupid police interrogations, or questioning by judges and lawyers, and not even the advice of lawyer friends who, with a serious and pompous look on their face, would tell him to leave everything in their hands. No fucking way, in their hands. Life was the killer, and he'd simply made certain that Sarita didn't suffer anymore from the deterioration of an illness or the immoral existence that the medical system was able to provide, while it racked up the charges. Sarita was barely forty-five years old, but now she was just a little lifeless piece of shit, a shell, nothing but skin and bones, a body without feeling that had no reason or purpose to continue breathing.

That's why he made a deal with himself, and swallowed the last gram of guilt, staying cool and competent the entire time.

18.

He sits down on the inn's porch, facing the street and the beach and thinks about Gombrowicz, who believed that writers were literature's greatest enemies. He's been reading the memoir of the Polish author who was known to say that seeing writers congregate in groups, like members of a union, made him feel nauseous. And Bruno Fólner also, he says to himself, speaking in the third person. You just know nothing good's going to come from that. It happened to me so many times on the reservation that it just left me feeling bitter. He had a reputation of being a surly old man, annoying, even hostile, but was just protecting himself, he justifies, that is, so as not to feel obligated to submit to the pressure of writing prologues and blurbs for book covers for lousy poets and wannabe short story writers in the village. Something like that. Someone should write an essay about the irritating effects that come from requests to write texts out of obligation. One should protect the solitude of the creative process and respect the absolute freedom of reading. Down with guilds, unions, associations, workshops, and even literary magazines, what the hell, after all, writing is the work of loners, ferocious wolves and hungry lionesses.

He doesn't know what to do about the anger he feels. On the table, the red Moleskine is as dead as the pig whose leg was cured to make the ham in the sandwich he doesn't eat.

The problem is, Fólner, he thinks with harshness, is you're fed up with your own limitations, your pathological insecurity when it comes to writing. That's it.

Anger has a name, after all.

He lets out a deep sigh, and thinks about Sarita, and his eyes tear up. He needs to weep over her; he always believed crying does a person good. That's what he used to tell the kids, when they were kids. And now he's alone and can cry; that porch is high and deserted enough to witness such a scene, like Faulkner's porches, the real Faulkner. For example, the *pinche porche* in *As I Lay Dying*, he murmurs in Mexican Spanish.

Fólner, he says to himself, as if secretly to the splendid morning that is such a contradiction, stop fucking around, Fólner, Bruno Fólner. And he repeats his new name to himself as he closes the notebook and cries. He simply cries like someone who lets tears pour down a drain.

The soft weeping, takes him by surprise. It shatters him for a few seconds, or minutes, an indefinite amount of time.

Then he goes down the stairs that lead to the sand, like an old man, conscious of each step.

He crosses the road and walks wearily along the boardwalk, forcing himself to clear away the pain, the guilt, and the anger.

It's not always cowardly to fight back tears.

Although he doesn't exactly know what the hell else it is.

19.

He sees her for the third time on the fifth night, after having a steak and salad for dinner, accompanied by two glasses of a decent 2005 Trapiche Merlot, and then settling into a deck chair on the front porch of the hotel to gaze at the sea, and the incredible moon above. He feels a bit anxious and thinks how much he'd like to smoke a cigarette at that very moment. He hasn't smoked for twenty years, but the desire returns at times, unvanquished. Oh, how he'd like a Cuban Romeo and Julieta cigar right now. Then the urge passes, luckily it passes.

Then he gets up and walks toward the sand with what could be considered a youthful stride; you seem like a kid, Fólner, he thinks, reassuring himself. Perhaps the anxiousness he feels comes from having written a couple pages that afternoon, but they weren't able to calm his nerves. Nothing extraordinary, barely a sketch of what could become a short story. He also took a siesta, a little under an hour, and before that, he read a biography of Jorge Amado and several poems by Drummond de Andrade, sensing that Brazilian literature, read there, opened its arms like someone who waits for you at the end of a journey. The journey to the journey that literature is. Literature itself as a journey. I wrote that in a novel, he reminds himself, noticing his restlessness.

He rolls up his pants, takes off his sandals, and walks along the beach. As the sand gently rubs the callouses on the soles of his feet, connecting his body to the earth, he feels an old sensual pleasure. He wonders what would happen if he kept walking to infinity, if he never returned to Praia Macacos, or to any place he'd left behind. To be an eternal wanderer like my grandfather, who was a train inspector and traveled all over the country; or like my old man who was a sailor. They used to say in my family that I'd be a pilot or an astronaut. I ended up being a writer, which is another kind of voyager. But I would've liked to have been so many other things: philosopher, wizard, linguist, or entertainer. Perhaps an evangelist, preacher, astrologer, broadcast mystic, alchemist, lone ranger, a German composer from the romantic period. He laughs, letting himself get carried away by old familiar fantasies. Why not a social scientist, prophet, Trotskyist, medieval troubadour, professor of semiotics, Carlos Gardel impersonator, perpetual student of psychology. Ha! I would've loved to have been a mediocre poet who suddenly — while still alive, that is — catapults to fame and doesn't know how to act. Or better yet, a brain surgeon, middleweight boxer, serial fornicator, bomber, fencer on the Olympic stage, counterfeiter, faith healer, consort of queens, clandestine glutton in the royal kitchen, NBA basketball player, expert witness, a mountain climber in Andorra.

He grins from ear to ear as he remembers that game, and others from his childhood they also used to play, at home, with Sarita and the kids. The most beautiful and outlandish profession was the one Marina came up with one night: a seamstress who sews gold buttons once we get to Mars. And Tomi's, when he was five-years-old: I want to be a blue cat that flies like Superman. They were happy, dreaming and laughing, surrounded by so much green and so many birds. Everything around them was the image of a perfect place in the world, and they were there, carefree and serene.

Two adjectives, says Bruno Fólner to himself, that fit perfectly the woman strolling down the boardwalk, in front of the Pousada da Baleia, beautiful and restrained, like a white gust of wind. He recognizes her and she intrigues him. She's too mysterious, too attractive not to perturb whoever sees her, especially if that someone is a guy of flesh and blood, like him, like me, he says, who feels as vulnerable as a thistle in the rain. He follows her with his gaze until she slips into the darkness, swiftly and elusively, like a bat.

He wants to call out to her, speak to her, but doesn't dare. He makes a false move, then freezes. In that instant, he concedes that if a man can't follow through with his intentions and merely leaves footsteps in the sand, the best thing he can do, in the long and early hours of dawn, is to imagine he's learning to fly like seagulls. That way he can get lost at sea and drown once and for all.

He decides to approach her, but a noisy truck distracts him. After it passes, she's no longer there. He searches for her, but knows right away it's useless. He feels a strange combination of curiosity, desire, and even a certain intellectual interest. He thinks that, in a way, she fits Bill Burroughs's memorable and misogynistic description: that woman was a fish; cold, slippery and hard to catch.

It's as if she's the one always calling the shots, which doesn't please him, but does attract him.

And then he sees her again, a white silhouette in the shadows. And he walks toward her feeling the lingering warmth of the sand between his toes, as he tries to convince himself that the best thing he could do right now is write the novel he's been contemplating. He'd promised himself he'd begin that very night, after returning from the beach and having coffee, followed by bourbon.

But then she appeared before him. Ghostly and emphatic.

Bruno Fólner recalls the words of the poet: "Sweet ghost, why are you visiting me...?"

And he walks toward her.

20.

That other early morning, not so long ago, and hours before dawn broke, he left the hospital through a side door without being seen. He'd obsessed over that detail and had confirmed, without a doubt, no one used that door, crossing its threshold discreetly several times during the last weeks, even before making the decision. That door lead to a kind of little square teeming with old orange and lemon trees, under whose thick canopy were cement benches that only in the morning welcomed the frightened rumps of relatives and friends who endured, anxious and tense, the slow passing of anguishing hours of surgery.

After crossing the little plaza, guaranteed to be empty, discreet, and silent at those hours, he left through another door, a much wider double door, which was always open, and lead to the parking lot reserved for doctors. Beyond that was an iron gate, which was never locked, and that no one passed through between midnight, when the garbage truck passed by, and five in the morning, when the first shift of nurses started to arrive.

He left through there, walking without being seen, especially because he'd taken the precaution to wear a black shirt and black pants. He made it to his car, parked three blocks away from the hospital, and in a few minutes left the city and headed for Route 11 on the way to Formosa. He knew exactly where he was going: in two and a half hours, he was in Puerto Pilcomayo, where ferry boats crossed the Paraguay River to Itá Enramada, starting at seven-thirty in the morning.

He abandoned his car on the Argentine side and crossed, contemplating the calm waters at that early hour. Halfway across the river, he threw his old Mac into the swirling eddies stirred up by the propellers, and on the other side, took a taxi to the bus station in Asunción, arriving before nine. He had breakfast in a café and got on a bus destined for Encarnación. He arrived in the early afternoon and transferred to another bus that took him to Ciudad del Este. There he stayed in the Hotel Líbano, a fairly decent three-star hotel that wasn't bustling or in the center of town, and after dinner, he made inquiries, with the guys at the hotel, about securing an impeccable passport to cross into Brazil.

The next morning, the chubby bellboy, smiling like a moderator of a business conference, gave him precise and very discreet instructions. It cost him two thousand dollars, which he had to pay in cash in advance, they asked him what name he wished to use from that moment on, and they handed it to him shortly after noon. By then, he'd contracted a cab driven by a young, grinning Palestine named Hassán, who at the border crossing between Paraguay and Brazil, greeted the cops and immigration agents from both countries the way you'd say hello to friends in the neighborhood you play soccer with twice a week. Hassán got them to stamp the passport with a special residency permit for an indefinite period of time, for the reasonable price of another two hundred dollars.

In Foz do Iguaçú, he went directly to the airport. He checked out flights to Cuiabá with a connection in Lima, and made reservations in the name of the person he'd been for sixty-four years in Argentina, the one he'd also decided to kill at daybreak the previous morning. In a travel agency inside the airport, he bought a ticket to Mexico via São Paulo, with the same old first and last name. And finally, in the office of TAM Airlines, he paid cash for a ticket in the name of Bruno Fólner, the owner of the brand spanking new passport, for the flight to Fortaleza via Rio de Janeiro, which was departing at four o'clock in the afternoon. And in the duty free shop, he purchased a new Mac that he'd set up on the plane. He'd throw away the flash drive later in a trash can.

21.

"Rejane, her name is Rejane," said Jorginho. He repeats it one or two more times: "Rejane. Rejane."

"Her name is Rejane? How do you spell that?"

"Re-ja-ne," Jorginho spells it out.

"So then it must be Re-Jane, like in English."

Jorginho explains that in Portuguese it's "Reyani," written the way you'd pronounce "Reyein," but it's not a name in English.

And he pronounces it again, "Re-ya-ni," accentuating the initial "r" with a guttural "g," that is "Gueyani."

"Gueyani," mimics Bruno Fólner, nodding his head. "Like the French pronunciation; the way Cortázar spoke . . . Gueyani. Lovely, sounds nice. And what's her story?"

Jorginho dries some glasses with a white cloth and doesn't respond. He continues his task, concentrating like a scientist at a microscope.

Bruno Fólner doesn't belabor the matter, acting as if he'd never asked anything.

And he recalls the first time, when he saw her off in the distance, the way you barely notice a shadow crossing the street. What he did notice was her dress, so dazzling white, strapless, and billowing from the waist down. It seemed she was walking barefoot, or perhaps wearing sandals that were also white, or maybe yellow, but at any rate a color as light as that clothed specter, which was what he thought of her at first sight. The shadow disappeared as it turned the corner of the hotel, as if absorbed by the night, leaving him thinking, what kind of woman could she be, one capable of grabbing his attention so intensely.

That happened the second night he was at the Pousada da Baleia, while having dinner and looking out at the bay, lost in thought. That night the sea appeared somewhat voluptuous, as if unappeased, and upon its surface the lights of the town shimmied like silver threads dancing gracefully in the wind. That time he didn't ask questions or make comments, but he did the following night, when it seemed that the woman was crossing the boardwalk from the opposite sidewalk in front of the inn, entering and leaving immediately, headed toward the center of town. Bruno Fólner discovered then that in fact she was barefoot, and even though he saw her from a distance, those feet appeared sensual to him.

"Beautiful woman," he said to Jorginho, certain he knew who she was.

"Oh, yes, Rejane," the innkeeper agreed, looking at a painting on the wall facing the concierge table, with a somewhat sad and nostalgic expression on his face, before telling him that she had been the most beautiful woman in Fortaleza: *"Ela foi a mais bela das mulheres de Fortaleza."*

Bruno Fólner wondered why he'd never noticed that painting, which didn't seem to be a work of much value. It was a typical seashore painting, full of breaking waves in blue, white and silver hues, with the eye-catching detail in the bottom right of a woman emerging from the sea with her jet black hair tangled in a whirlwind of waves and rough water, or so it seemed. Her face couldn't be seen clearly, but her shiny tousled hair stood out. Had he noticed that painting before, Bruno Fólner said to himself, he would've thought it was a cheap reproduction, a worthless print like those you see in hotels all over the world. Yet now he was intrigued.

"So what's her story?" he repeated, but didn't get an answer because at that very moment Dona Amalia called out to her husband from the kitchen.

22.

Throughout the following day, silence reigns, as dense and persistent as the surging sea off in the distance. Only a couple of cars and a motorcycle disrupt the perfection of the afternoon.

It's Sunday and the sea's a bit choppy. Just right for a few *mates*, thought Bruno Fólner, who had drifted off in the deck chair after lunch, like a retiree snoozing in a plaza. After rousing, he picked up the newspaper, yesterday's *O Globo*, and paged through it at random. Next he picked up the notebook and jotted down some ideas, then looked out at the sea and the cloudy sky and scribbled some more notes, and at one point the thought crossed his mind that time, like life in Mexico, wasn't worth a thing.

He's been sitting quite a while on the porch, which looks out at the sea wall, drinking a bourbon that Caio brought him, diluted with lots of ice, a splash of soda water, and a slice of lemon, while thinking he'd be better off staying clear of certain recurring memories: the moment he unplugged the respirator without hesitating; the gentle waves of the Paraguay River seen from the ferry; the snoring of the fat guy reeking of beer who sat next to him on the flight from Foz to Río.

The bourbon brings back memories of his college days, when he believed being a professor of literature could be a wonderful thing. That afternoon he wrote a few pages on the topic, knowing they won't amount to anything, but he dashed them off as a way of distracting himself from the main content in the notebook, which now rests open on the wicker table, right beneath his chin. That Moleskine was given to him by Luis Sepúlveda at a writers' conference in Asturias. Some scatterbrained editor had invited him to Gijón, where he'd dined on some delicious lobster with Luis and his buddies, a bunch of fat, loud-mouthed party animals. He also took an interest in the life of Corín Tellado, with whom he'd had coffee one long unforgettable afternoon in the Café Dindurra, on the Paseo de Begoña. None of that is in the Moleskin, but it does exist in his memory. He only participated in a couple round tables, and then traveled, first to Salamanca and afterwards to Ávila, where he gave a few readings organized by that editor. The failure of sales for the two books he published in Spain was as impressive as it was swift, and he was left forever with the feeling that if that editor hadn't purchased a round-trip ticket, he would've left him stranded there.

The Moleskine is one of his most prized souvenirs from that trip and now he goes back to writing notes in it for what he supposes, imagines, or wants to suppose or imagine, will be that novel he'll later transcribe to the Mac.

"Either there is no story, or he doesn't want to tell it to me," he whispers to himself a little later, while finishing the bourbon and savoring the pleasure he always gets from sucking the ice at the end.

As if he'd heard him, Jorginho puts down the cloth after drying the last glass for the eleventh time, and goes over to the table on the porch, grabs the back of a chair and turns it around to sit backwards, as if protecting himself. He places his hands on the top rail, and sadness comes over him once again, when he says in Portuguese: "Rejane, doesn't have a story, *Senhor* Bruno, she is the story."

23.

Of course I'm not going to kill myself. I'm Bruno Fólner, and since a few days ago, that's how I identify myself, and though I'm not overjoyed, I can live with myself. I've always been a very passionate guy, energetic, active, and restless my entire life. Suited for politics, they used to say, when a few friends wanted me to throw my hat into that arena. No way. It's true I'm as agitated as an anthill, and relentless and adamant about my convictions, but there's no chance I'd commit suicide now. I'd suffer like a pig first, before making the cowardly move to abandon the game, much less end it over an impossible quest for a utopian well-being. Perhaps take a shot at something else, if it suits me, but keep to the edge, grasping at murky lifelines, while navigating dangerous abysses, real and palpable.

Once again, he remembers Leopoldo Lugones, whose suicide suddenly takes on meaning. Obviously, he's not thinking about committing suicide, not at all, but it's also true that if Lugones shows up and hangs around. . .
For years, many other suicides have intrigued him: Horacio Quiroga in the instant he drank the cup of cyanide; Alfonsina Storni walking into the sea never to return; Tadeo Ronzini, the next-door-neighbor kid, who was completing his military service, and while on leave one Sunday, blew his brains out with one shot of a Mauser. Also that young municipal employee from Buenos Aires who passed himself off as the mayor and called a press conference, and once everyone had gathered, stuck the barrel of a shotgun in

his mouth and fired, leaving his brains imprinted on the flag, the wall, and part of the ceiling.

But it's not suicide that matters to him, rather death. That fucking indescribable goddess who pursues him.

He looks up and sees Jorginho. He winks at him as a sign of naive complicity that the man accepts. That's what usually happens, just try winking at someone. Instantaneous connection. A feeling of relief, respite from loneliness. Something like that.

Jorginho washes a glass he's already washed and decides to change the music. He puts on an old CD of Milton Nascimento. Then removes it and goes back a few more years in time, playing one of Elis Regina, much to my surprise. That kind of nostalgia is hard to believe in such a young guy. Jorginho was just a kid when Elis killed herself. The Queen of Bossa Nova, sensual and with that incomparable voice, checked herself out. Overdosed, who are they kidding? She ingested cocaine and Tamezepam up the wazoo, and was drunk to boot, liters of alcohol, and bim, bam, boom, to hell with life.

It's an option, Bruno Fólner admits, but extreme, he adds.

"I'll have a whisky, please," he orders looking up, and suddenly realizing there's someone on the other side of the glass, outside the window. It's Rejane. And she seems to be looking at him, or at least that's what he thinks.

I should go out and speak to her, he says to himself, but doesn't move.

The one who does move and brings him a bottle, glass, and ice is Laurinha, Jorginho's sister. Thin, tall, and busty, she's a beauty with dark skin like polished onyx. She can't be more than fifteen years old, but already two perfect lemons are sprouting from her chest. Glistening as if a private moon were condemned to follow her forever, Laurinha knows only one word in Spanish and loves to repeat it: "*Mogollón*," "a lot," a word with multiple meanings, like shitload, mess or jam, hustle, but a term not used in Argentine Spanish. "You like it, Laurinha?" And she replies, "*Mogollón*" and laughs revealing the inside of her mouth, red like a pomegranate.

"Do you know what that word means?" he asked her the other morning after breakfast.

"*Sim, mogollón é muito*," she responded. "Yes, *mogollón* means a lot," explaining further in delightful Portuguese: "It has to do with quantity, an enormous amount, the biggest idea of something."

"Only when it comes to love, Laurinha, in Mexico they say *mogollón* when you love someone completely. You'll learn that when you're older."

"*Amor é sempre total, Senhor Bruno. Ou não é amor.*"

The girl loaded the tray with dirty dishes and returned to the kitchen, smiling and proud as *La Flor de la Canela* over her retort, "love is always complete, or it's not love." He watched her walk away, gliding in a pair of flip-flops, two sizes too big for her feet that squeaked cha-cha, cha-cha with each step she took.

He observes her again, with admiration but without lust, like a grandfather: the perfect back, her cute ass like a melon mold jiggling beneath her green mini-skirt. Barely fifteen years old, my God, just imagine what she'll be like at twenty, he thinks, and turns to the bright window, which Rejane has abandoned to take her place like a statue, on the boardwalk, on the other side of the avenue, over there, facing the sea and gazing at the vastness like an astronomer scanning the sky.

He fills his glass with an affordable White Horse scotch over lots of ice, and drinks nearly all of it in two gulps, then stands up, thinking, that ripe fruit is also sadly beyond his reach.

Then once again he recalls the poetry of Drummond de Andrade:
My heart does not know.
Foolish, ridiculous, and fragile is my heart.

24.

He felt no guilt as he gazed at Sarita, dead. He stroked her cheek lovingly, caressed her mouth, and traced the contours of her face. He noticed he was more emotional than what he'd expected, as if gauging too late and in vain what he'd just done. Then he looked down at his hands and felt the same old disgust. Ever since he was a boy, he chewed his fingernails, his entire life, especially the cuticles, which always looked raw. His fingers seemed shorter, atrophied at the blunt tips, pure flesh edging the old nail beds that had become rough and calcified from so much biting and salivating. The damage was irreparable, just like the harm to his soul.

He's had breakfast and is drinking one last cup of coffee. He looks out at the sea and thinks about *San La Muerte*, the little skeleton who stands with a scythe in his right hand, the saint they turn to in Northeast Argentina, for assistance and protection. In his former life, he himself wrote about a guy who gets out of jail and has the little saint beneath his skin. A tiny little saint, a millimeter carved out of human bone with the tip of a knife. According to tradition, the little skeleton must be made of human bone in order for the miniscule saint to be effective, infallible, miraculous. Then it's inserted under the skin at knifepoint, into the chest or bicep, and it becomes a habit to rub the little saint while speaking, as if to call on him in times of need.

How he'd like to have one of those now, thinks Bruno Fólner, staring at the cup. Before that was his name, back when he was G.R., the day he carried out his decision, he'd thought even then about Saint Death. Or perhaps it was before, he thinks now, beginning with the day he started to plan the elimination of his wife. He was far away, in Salta, where he'd given a seminar at the Universidad Nacional, and connected with Sarita by Skype that night. She responded with a strange voice, like someone covering up pain, and she didn't want the camera on, saying she preferred to just speak and listen, and it was obvious that speaking was difficult. Her discomfort was undeniably intense and her physical decline advanced. Her deterioration was due to her own negligence. She'd always been a rebellious patient, careless, and after years of naively believing herself to be eternal, now she was paying the consequences of avoiding medical exams, tests, check-ups. All that perturbed him, infuriated him: he'd tried all manner of persuasion, but it almost always ended in a screaming match. Don't be so irresponsible with your health; take care of yourself, God damn it, we need you healthy. The marital spats were based on that disagreement: you have to see a doctor and do what he tells you; I'll go when I feel like it and can go, don't order me around; and the insults would escalate like milk boiling in a pot. He'd get fed up and leave, slamming the door behind him, well then, up and die, you crazy fool, and she'd go back to her indifference and evasiveness, as if wagering that time could pass as Lewis Carroll would've imagined, but for watches designed by Escher. There was no other way to explain that absurdity: he in his sixties and healthy, albeit obsessive and overprotective; and she young and condemned, denying the worst and wasting away, hour by hour. Until suddenly, she petered out and turned into a thing that only breathes. Who can explain this bullshit to me, not God or the fucking bitch, the man that now called himself Bruno Fólner would say to himself.

Of course all that is over. End of the movie; reality is different. I should think about other things, change the subject once and for all. Calculate, for example, the size of the universe. Or of hell, just like Galileo facing the Florentine academia.

Don't screw me over, he says to himself, after Dona Amalia informs him that Jorginho tried but couldn't find bourbon, no Maker's Mark in all of Praia Macacos, *nem Maker's Mark, em tudo Praia Macacos.*

25.

As he crosses the avenue, he admits being incapable of distinguishing if it's desire or something else that woman arouses in him. It must be or something else, he thinks, because my desire is on hold. Today I wouldn't know how to figure out what's happened to my libido. For months, my sex drive has been a sleeping beauty. The call of the flesh and other clichés are little more than memories because Sarita took all that with her too. But now, this very mysterious woman rekindles at least his curiosity, like a renewal of interest, not yet of appetite, or who knows.

He stands next to her and looks out at the infinite dark blue night. He's been writing or reading all day long, and upon seeing her, he crossed the road, determined to approach her, but not sure why, perhaps out of pure curiosity. It's not just her body he finds irresistible: so curvaceous and yet graceful, seemingly firm, sensitive, and delicate, and barely concealed beneath her white dress that sways in the sea breeze. No, it's not desire he feels; neither is it sorrow for desire that's dead and gone. It's more like an undefinable nostalgia. That's all he can clearly pinpoint. Nostalgia for something, nothing more.

He stands beside her, but unfazed, she doesn't look at him.

"¿A Senhora Rejane?"

"¿E o Senhor?"

"Bruno Fólner," he responds with a feeling of liberation from something, as if saying his new name out loud were a declaration of beginnings. Exactly that, he thinks, a fresh start.

Neither of them says a word. All that can be heard is the persistence of the unrelenting surf. And they stay that way for some time.

"*O amor é sempre total ou não é amor*," whispers Bruno Fólner suddenly, barely projecting his voice over the sound of the breaking waves.

The woman doesn't react, not even with a gesture.

"I heard that from the mouth of fifteen-year-old girl . . ."

The woman waits a few seconds, as if processing the words, "love is always complete, or it's not love."

"*¿O Senhor é poeta?*"

Bruno Fólner smiles. She has a beautiful low voice, a deep contralto. We're all poets when sadness overcomes us, or forgetting hurts us, he thinks, and feels like saying, but says nothing.

"No. I have only memories," he tells her in Spanish. *Saudades*, yearnings that no longer matter.

"*Isso*," "that's it," she says, elongating the "I" as if chanting in a litany.

And they remain silent, both of them gazing at the sea in an almost religious stance, like believers before an altar at a midnight mass.

26.

On another splendid morning, Bruno Fólner reads *El Sol del Chaco* carefully and realizes they don't know a thing. Or that's how it seems, he says to himself, there's not a single comment or hint, no trace. It's just a matter of not going crazy. That's it: immediately he confirms he will not go insane, because even supposing they don't look for him, he refuses to accept the possibility that his crime had been met with approval. He's scoured the internet in a thousand ways, all morning long, and no newspaper, no site, no search for names produced results. And yet, it's hard for him to believe it. Everything was left in clear sight, he reasons, so that when they found Sarita's body, they would've seen all the evidence pointed to me as the one who hastened her death, to put it properly and delicately.

Now all that's left to do is cross his fingers that they'll forget about him, or better still, that they'll not look or wait for him. That's obvious, but that kind of factual silence disturbs him. All his email accounts have been closed. He doesn't want to read emails that would increase his own anxiety, and he tries to convince himself that he doesn't want to know more, although perhaps he should've left one account active, or should open a new one, or not, for what reason, better not . . . No, he doesn't know, but it's always best not to make hasty decisions. That's one of his rules. He's an outsider in the world now, and will be for some time, more like for all time, a sort of forever. I know very well all this is selfish and fucked, but that's how it is; the kids would probably ask for explanations, place demands on me, and blame me, because in spite of all the merciful justifications, I did kill their mother. Hell, what child would put up with that. It's a fine mess, that's what it is. I'd be better off finishing the novel I started and sending it to the agency. A PDF from whatever fake Hotmail or Yahoo, and chau. They'll know what to do, and if later there are royalties, the kids can collect them. For that very reason, I put all the powers of attorney in order. And enough of this.

He orders tea with lemon that Laurinha brings him with her shuffling cha-cha, cha-cha and her cute boobs bulging under her t-shirt. He looks at her and smiles with gratitude like a naughty old codger who's no longer hot to trot, but content to take in the view, and convinced of the magical effect of literature. Or that's what he believes, or wants to believe: cling to writing and put an end to certain fantasies. Because it's clear that if he could be with Laurinha, buck naked, he'd be able to resuscitate completely the man he used to be. Sixtyish but not dead, he says to himself and smiles. Dirty old man, keep your hands to yourself.

A perfect morning, Bruno, for trying to believe.

27.

The encounter is magical, or so it seems. Magic is a cliché, but those old sayings often come to our aid. And are welcome, he thinks, while observing her and not making a move because Rejane is right there, and if anyone's going to do something, she'll be the one. She'll do everything or nothing at all.

Magic like a gleaming point, shifting and symbolic, he thinks, but of what, he wonders, symbolic of what. And he watches her do nothing, because Rejane is a statue and he too is frozen. What must it be like to do everything? Willfully, and, perhaps, out of necessity. Hers, because I'm just a cool bystander, an instrument, a companion who won't screw you over. True, I did suggest we talk about ourselves, our lives, although with certain deception — on my part — knowing my story was partial, as indeed it's turning out to be, and therefore false, foolishly sugar-coated in my favor.

But it doesn't matter to her, or she acts like it doesn't; or maybe it was just that she kept her guard up because her grief was so intense, or still is.

No, I'm telling it all wrong.

At one point, she took my hand. Or did I take hers, I don't know, it doesn't matter. We held hands and I felt something stir inside. Her hand seemed somewhat masculine, soft to the touch, but with a powerful grip as firm as steel. It was like the hand that waits for you at the border and determines if you cross, or not, upon arrival.

I'm sorry if I don't know how to be less confusing.

I didn't recognize my desires, if I had them, and of course I had them, and I felt great and loved being attached to that magnificent female. Although I'm not, or not anymore, a macho toward anyone, I felt attractive and charming, while she held my hand. Clear communion, the strength of intimacy in that clasp of hands.

Her story overwhelmed me. I close my eyes and I'm still overcome. It flows through me like a deluge, sinks into my skin like an incisor, severing me, before reviving and restoring me. She said she didn't need to tell or share anything, but *simplesmente,* that's how she said it, *simples-mente,* as they say in Portuguese, combining simplicity and thought, she'd found me appealing. Or not exactly me, but the way I looked at her. Your gaze vibrates like the strings of a *berimbau,* she said in that clear and soft Portuguese that allowed me to understand her perfectly, you look at me like someone who keeps a secret. And she had her own. And the weight of a secret can be, at times, unbearable. That's how she put it, unbearable, and I agreed with a nod. And she added that she had loved very much a marvelous man, like no other, "*O Marco,*" she called him, captain of a small shrimp boat, the *Flamingo,* that he'd take out to sea every morning at dawn.

She took a long silent pause, crystalline and delicate, not a dramatic silence, the grave and heavy kind, no, this one was a serene silence, almost gentle, that also seemed to reverberate, oddly enough, like an echoing note of that Brazilian musical bow, the *berimbau.* And then she continued, saying that she used to wait for him on this very beach, at this very spot, showing that imaginary space with her outstretched hands. And she'd greet him from the bay, and when he saw her, he'd sound the horn of the *Flamingo,* filling the air with its raucous duo of trumpets. And then, as he entered the port, she'd help him with the mooring lines and leap on board and they'd embrace and kiss. She'd help the crew unload and finally Marco would cover the motor with an old leather cape and they'd go ashore together, and that's how it was. Later, they'd swim for a while and play in the water, celebrating the happiness and sustenance the sea bestowed upon them, then they'd eat something, walk along the sea wall and the boardwalk until dusk, only to frolic once again in the sea, on the other side of the bay, sometimes naked, like dolphins, and they'd make love, then lie beneath the palm trees, talking and dreaming, and end the day dining by moonlight, before retiring because the next day, and each and every day, they obeyed the mandates of love by affirming and repeating the pristine serenity of that perfect life.

"And then?" he asks, sensing as if he already knows the rest of the story, which inevitably must end badly, in tragedy.

Rejane maintains a long and calm silence, finally murmuring:

"Then what they must have already told you happened..."

Bruno Fólner sighs deeply, his mind blank.

"No. No one told me anything. I asked, but no answers."

She looks out at the sea, and he looks at her looking at the sea. Her eyes have a strange glimmer that Bruno barely detects, observing her from the side the way horses glance. Rejane's lips move, as if saying something in silence, but he can't tell if it's a story or a song. He fine tunes his ears and can barely hear her. Rejane recounts in few words, and without facts or dates or geographic details: it was all beautiful and perfect until the morning that a storm at sea, a ferocious hurricane, battered the *Flamingo*, and it never returned. She had asked him not to go out that day, not to sail into the sea, telling him the clouds were a bad omen. Perhaps she even lied about a disturbing dream, she can't remember. But she did beg him in a thousand ways not to set sail that morning, not to leave the bay.

A longer silence follows, much heavier, impenetrable. *O Marco*, she whispers, didn't heed the bad forecast, stubborn and defiant as he was. He left at daybreak, as he did each dawn, swiftly and so handsome. No damned storm, and he had weathered many, was going to set him back. Etcetera. And he didn't return. As was to be expected, said Rejane, without letting her voice falter. He didn't return. None of the three shrimp boats that went out that morning returned.

Then Bruno Fólner extends his hand. Without forethought or intent, he raises his right hand spontaneously and searches in the air for Rejane's left hand. Unexpressed solidarity, he says to himself and thinks, unaware he's thinking, or what he's thinking, earnest gesture of solitude, beacon in the storm, faint flare, and then it drops. The hand drops, unclasped.

Only Chico Andrade survived, she says, and barely, how ironic, Chico, an old man, made it to the shore the next day because he did the only thing you can do in a storm: cling to a plank and float effortlessly, without wasting energy. Chico floated and the sea brought him after the gale, along with pieces of the boats, some torn sails, a useless pail, a sneaker, mute testimonies of the misfortunate shipwrecked sailors. And Old Chico said that the *Flamingo* held on longer than the others, that Marco's prowess was extraordinary, and that the boat endured those turbulent waters until suddenly it began to sink out at sea, quickly and fatally, as if it had been seized by the Devil, and vanished.

Bruno feels a light squeeze, then a shifting of her hand, as if that hand controlled his without letting go of it. The double fist they form remains tight when she whispers that then, before Chico finishes his story, she rushes to look for him, excellent swimmer that she is, she dives into the sea and swims against the waves and the sound of the town, and perhaps against the fury of God and searches for him desperately, swimming desperately to the mouth of the bay, to the middle of nowhere, swimming and swimming until she drifts out to sea.

28.

He always believed he was a better writer than what his measly fame gave him credit for. He knew, of course, that's exactly what nearly all writers in the world think. No one talks about it, but you can bet that's what they all think. It certainly was his way of thinking, when he was G.R.

And Bruno Fólner laughs to himself, enjoying that intimate reflection, but not without some remorse, because he's aware his literary projects never amounted to much, and in fact, for some time now, deep inside, he'd admitted that his talent was of minor consequence. He was not destined to write a magnificent work, and to a certain point, he'd given up on the idea. Literature the world over had gone downhill, and what's more, writing had become a shoddy stab at importance, a contest for far too competitive egos, cheap reads as fleeting as a sandbank, and he didn't belong in that arena, although as fate would have it, some of his books had been published. He'd come to the conclusion there were too many writers in the world. An excess. Fast-spreading plague. And few great poets. The world was fucked.

Years ago things were different, Bruno Fólner says to himself while looking at the sea.

Well, years ago everything was different, and I was G.R., a young Latin American with prospects, he responds to himself. And he also says to himself, grimly, back then, twenty some years ago, Sarita lay on the sands of Honolulu, as luminous as a mother of pearl shell, but now she must be rotting away, one worm at a time.

At that moment, he hears a commotion outside. Like a door being slammed, strange and unusual, like a stray cannon shot. Immediately afterwards the telephone rings.

"Dom Bruno," says Dona Amalia softly. "*Aquí perguntam por o Senhor...*"

"Someone's asking for me? Who?"

"A man who says he's an immigration agent," she responds in Portuguese.

"I'm coming," he declares in Spanish, recognizing that all his senses are on high alert, and all the sirens in the world are blaring. "But what was that loud noise, Dona Amalia?"

"*Nada,*" she says laughing, and explains that it was just Caími who was clumsy and tripped over some cans in the kitchen. "*Desculpe... ¿O Senhor desce?*"

"Yes, I'll be down in a minute."

29.

The cyanide pill fell out when he pulled apart the roll of dollar bills he'd taken from the safe because he needed some *reales.* He'd forgotten that the same afternoon he made the decision to kill Sarita, he'd inserted it securely among the small piles of bills wrapped in rubber bands. When it fell to the floor just now, he simply watched it roll, until it came to a stop, next to a leg of the bed. And then he stared at in on the floor, as if examining a white ant, with a kind of analytical detachment.

He picks it up, raising his eyebrows and says, what the hell, you never know. It's a matter of proceeding carefully, he thinks, like a watchmaker, or as he imagines a watchmaker would proceed. He remembers Don Jacinto who lived on Edison Street, a cold guy with eyes that bulged like a toad's, perhaps a professional deformation, because he always seemed to look at everything with just one eye. That's how he observed the rolling pill, which seemed somewhat lethal to him. And he bends down and picks it up, and puts it back into the safe, no longer tucked away but loose, alone and deadly, like a tarantula. He doesn't know if he'll use it one day, if he'll ever have the courage to swallow it, and figures probably never, but it's good to keep it handy. The important lesson here is detachment, he says to himself next, as if to change the subject.

He's been thinking that at some point he should go to an ATM and take out cash, and perhaps this is the right moment, he says to himself, grabbing his passport and sticking three hundred dollars in the right pocket of his pants. It's better than changing money all the time. He'd asked Jorginho and he informed him there are two ATMs in Praia Macacos: one at the bus terminal and the other at the end of the opposite side of the bay, in the Petrobras gas station. He could walk there, whichever direction he chooses to go. But the problem is the ATMs leave trails. So better not, doesn't make sense, he thinks and chides himself for being impulsive. It's best to keep re-lying on Jorginho, who the first time he needed *reales*, exchanged them at a decent rate. He can exchange dollars for *reales* in modest amounts, as often as he likes, and with no questions asked, and that won't leave tracks. That's better than withdrawing Brazilian money from the machine, something he should do only in case of an emergency. And not in large quantities, or at the same ATM, rather, let's say a little at a time, be careful, he tells himself, decisively.

He has two accounts with substantial available funds, one in Spain and the other in Miami, in a gringo bank. He also brought checkbooks, but just in case, he says to himself, because they're easy to trace. Although you never know. Before killing Sarita, he took the precaution of canceling the delivery of any information by postal service and converted all his accounts exclusively to on-line. He simply mentioned to the kids that he'd closed them and no longer had foreign bank accounts. And he even declared the same to the AFIP, the Argentine Federal Revenue Service, lying that the accounts were no longer open. So all's well, he thinks, cautioning himself that with-drawals from ATMs leave traceable evidence. He'll dip into those funds if he needs them one day, but for now it's best to keep those accounts frozen, the same for all the cards. He has enough dollars in bills, and he has Jorginho to change moderate amounts whenever he needs *reales*. So all's well. There's an order for things and it's just a matter of following it.

He goes into the bathroom saying to himself that the guy downstairs can wait. His passport and residency visa are impeccable. He washes his hands recalling that he bought the cyanide pill from El Gordo Núñez the same day he started thinking he'd kill Sarita. I found him in the Bar La Es-trella, where he's a daily fixture, and I invited him to have coffee and chat about the old fucked up times of the dictatorship. El Gordo Núñez never turns down such an invitation because he loves to talk about his days as a militant. He was part of the guerrilla group, the *Montoneros*, and near the end of the dictatorship, was imprisoned for a while and released in 1983, enjoying a certain prestige that eroded over the years, following the return of democracy. And of course, he himself contributed to the erosion of that status with his own apathy and pathological lying. And it didn't take long for his old comrades-in-arms to denounce him as a coward, a chicken shit who'd tremble at the mere possibility of having to think for himself. That type of adventure was too much for him, a wimp who seemed like a character straight out of Sergio Pitol's stories.

Now, some thirty years later, El Gordo Núñez is a pathetic character in the city. Not only is he mediocre, completely incapable of succeeding at anything, but his greatest pursuit was not to pursue anything useful, and to live off the pension of his mother, who's very old now. Solid gray would be the only color on a Pantone paint strip to describe him, and his only virtue would be his life-long ability to deceive people.

In the Bar La Estrella he's a bit of an icon, a low-down tightwad, always on the lookout for someone who will pay attention to him, buy him coffee, or gin. I did all three things and steered the conversation to the myth of the cyanide pills that militants used to kill themselves when they were captured back in those ruthless times. El Gordo shot back that it wasn't a myth, that in fact, the organization provided them, and that many of his comrades had made the heroic decision not to give themselves up alive to the enemy. After bolting down the last drops of his second glass, he mentioned, in a low voice, that he still had the pill they'd given him and, then winked at me and said he'd be willing to sell it to me for a thousand bucks. That quickly sealed it for me that the guy was also slippery, a kind of scumbag, a piece of crap left over from a period full of futile heroism. I bought it from him for half the price, telling him I was collecting materials from that period for a museum to the thwarted revolution that some old buddies were mounting in Rosario. Both of us knew that was a lie, but neither of us cared.

Only now, as he placed it next to the neat bundles of dollars in the little safe recessed in the wall inside the wardrobe, did Bruno Fólner wonder if Núñez hadn't sold him any old pill, just one more piece of residual crap. Then he smiles, thinking he wasn't smart enough to even think of that. And he opens the door and goes down to the lobby.

30.

The interview with the guy from Immigration, to refer to him some way, seems to be a perfectly routine matter. The man, a lethargic fatso with yellow, tobacco-stained teeth, is seated at a table in the corner furthest from the bar and the big picture window. As soon as Bruno Fólner introduces himself, he greets him coolly and gestures for him to sit down across the table. He's positioned himself such that he's shaded from the light that filters in from outside and shines brightly on the face of the one he's about to interrogate.

First he clears his throat, while Bruno Fólner asks Caio very politely to bring him a *cafezinho*, before settling into the chair.

"It has come to our attention", begins Choppers, "that the *Senhor* is now residing in Praia Macacos." He takes a long pause and looks him square in the eye. Bruno Fólner sustains that stare without flinching. The fat ass leans back, like a treacherous evil pig in a kid's movie, and continues pronouncing in a smooth and somewhat monotone voice that given you have not declared your residency to the proper authorities, as is expected of all foreigners who are not in the country as tourists, I have come to inform you officially in the name of the Federal Government of Brazil that you must legalize your immigration status, and you have 48 hours to do so. And he extends a form stamped with an official seal for him to sign. Bruno Fólner reads it quickly and signs at the bottom. Please print your name and put your passport number. He does so and returns it, weighing whether the guy's just a pencil pusher who feels as important as a Roman emperor, or a miserable cop who's setting a trap for him.

"Can I see your passport?," asks the Pig, and Bruno Fólner hands it over and watches as the guy leafs through it, nods, and returns it just as Caími arrives with the coffee. Anything else you'd like to know? he asks while stirring the sugar. Not particularly, although we always want to know the future plans of immigrants; they'll ask you about that when you go to get your residency permit approved. I don't have any plans yet; I like this place, and maybe I'll stay, or maybe I'll leave. And how long do you plan to reside in Brazil? Impossible to say, because it seems I'm falling in love, and he tries out his best smile while looking the fatso in the eye. Oh yes, Brazil is a marvelous place to fall in love, but is the *Senhor* able to afford living in our country? I have a few years under my belt and some savings I hope will last until the good Lord calls me, he responds, betting five to one that the guy, like millions of Brazilians, is a believer or a fanatic of some sect or supposed religion. Choppers barely wags his big head affirmatively and struggles to stand up, as if all his gears were rusty. He states that Pousada da Baleia will be recorded as his legal permanent residence in the *República Federativa do Brasil*, and he recommends that he conduct himself properly and fall in love deeply. He said the latter with a wide and completely yellow, viperous smile. And without extending his hand to shake, he took his leave, pleased with himself.

So pleased with himself that Bruno Fólner feels as if the man had stuck a thorn stuck in his side.

31.

In this town, Dom Bruno, they've always said that Rejane came from the sea, Jorginho tells me, turning his head from side to side like an owl. For the first time he reminds me of The Gazers because his steely dry eyes stare without blinking. Black-chested eagles gaze that way too.

She came to Macacos years ago, and no one knows, or ever knew, how she ended up in this town, he goes on to say. That's just how it is in these little coastal towns; people just show up, one day they're not here, and the next day they are, just like you, like us, and no one asks too many questions. *Tudo bem.*

Some said she came from Algarve, Portugal, where she used to sing *fados* until she lost her voice. But someone else claimed she came from Porto Alegre, where she'd been a bartender in a brothel, until the day she got involved in some drug deal and paid the price with six years in Recife, in the penitentiary of Buen Pastor de Iputinga. Who knows.

Of course, many believe she was born in the sea and isn't human at all, while others argue she only swam in the sea to put an end to her life, you know, in small towns they say lots of things. People can't live without rumors, hearsay, gossip. Among the rumors that still circulate in this town, or should we say, stories that are invented, is the one that claims she escaped from a whorehouse on the Argentine border, between São Borja and Itaquí, cities on the banks of the Uruguay River, and left there by horseback, chasing after a circus tightrope walker, who died months later, after falling fifteen meters head first. Nearly all the tales link her to tragedy, as you can see: Rejane, mistress of death, stuff like that, popular fabrications. And there are others even more outrageous: that she escaped, but this time from an insane asylum in Santa Catarina, where she became the leader of a Batucada percussion group, and was given permission to perform sambas one 7th of September, our Independence Day, a celebration from which no patient returned. From there, she went to Manaus, following a knife thrower who'd outline her body with blades, until one day she stabbed him herself when she discovered him with a man, naked and panting beneath the lion tamer. And they also said, and used to say, those who told tales, that after that incident, rumor had it she traveled up the Amazon, until she came to the sea, making her way to São Luiz, where she hooked up with a businessman who married her and later sold her, well anyway, everyone knows that truth can always be uncertain, and when it's so twisted, it's even more difficult to establish.

Naturally, Jorginho concluded, all the rumors began with the same burning question: Why did she come to Praia Macacos? And there's always been just one natural and simple response: And why not?

What's certain is she started going at night to Lourenço Sarabia's bar and tavern called *O Bar dos Anjos,* the Two Angels Bar, because Lourenço is from Lisbon, from the Mouraria neighborhood, and is of African descent like nearly everyone around here. That bar sits where the sea wall begins, I don't know if you've been there, I hope not, it's not advisable. It's on this side, where the barges dock. And that's where she could be seen in the afternoon, that's for sure, I'm telling you Dom Bruno, I saw her with my own eyes. She'd stand there for no apparent reason, gazing at who knows what and with what longing until dusk, when she'd enter the bar as if looking for something, and no one knew what, but it wasn't, or didn't seem to be a person or food. Always with the strange sad expression and that unbridled resounding beauty. Who knows what she did inside, I never pay attention to gossip, but I saw her, I saw her there, many times. For sure.

Jorginho freshens Bruno Fólner's whisky and fixes himself another *caipirinha.* What is certain is that she never said a word about her past, whispers the innkeeper, sniffling as if he were catching a cold, or about to cry. Nor did she deny anything, never, nothing that was said, or that they still say, always acting like a person without a past, like someone who'd emerged from the sea, washed up by the waves, you've seen how the waves bring and take away things that were once alive? Well that's Rejane for you, appearing, time and time again, as always, like a twist of fate, fulfilled, as the saying goes.

And why does she always dress in white? asks Bruno, sucking a shard of ice after taking a sip.

No one in this entire town would say for certain if they saw her wear anything else, or perhaps it's just that it doesn't matter because it's so common here: many coastal women dress in white, ¿né? Flowing skirt, camisole, completely white, always, and at times the torso covered by shawls with braided fringe, white or very light colors. A classic vision of Praia Macacos, ¿né?

And Lourenço Sarabia? Or Marco?

It was actually Lourenço who brought his two brothers over: Zé Antonio, the older one, and Marquinho, the youngest. They made it to Macacos on a Dutch cargo ship, and because of them, the rumor got started that Rejane had been a singer of *fados* in Lisbon. She and Zé Antonio used to recite together the classic verses of Pessoa: "There are maladies worse than maladies, aches that do not ache, even in the soul, but those are more painful than the others." And all for loose change dropped into a hat by passersby and tourists, next to the Teatro Lírico and in front of Lisbon's Central Station. There he tried to woo her, showing off his seductive virtues, which, nonetheless, weren't enough because she fell madly in love with Marquinho and the brothers opted to keep the peace between them.

And then?

Rejane fell in love forever and seemed to be happy. Amalia and I liked to watch her sing and shriek with laughter, with that kind of infinite charm and seaside elegance, by that I mean her graceful way of walking and that beautiful voice of a lady from the Portuguese colonies of Africa.

So what's her true story?

Jorginho takes the last sip of his *caipirinha*, smiles enigmatically while casting his eagle eyes toward the sky, and then recites an amusing quatrain:

> A Portuguese was amazed to see
> That in their tender infancy,
> All the children of France
> Spoke French so fluently . . .

32.

He closes his laptop and stretches his arms back to loosen up. The afternoon recedes with a spectacular flourish, and he wonders about something he once read, not sure where, but fairly certain the idea came from Gombrowicz: at the height of the Cold War, and while living in exile in Paris, that extraordinary poet who was Czeslaw Milosz wrote that, at least at that time, the difference between an intellectual from the West and one from Eastern Europe was in essence quite simple: "the westerner has yet to have them shove something up his ass."

Of course, if he had to say that now, thinks Bruno Fólner laughing inside and lowering his arms, Milosz would amend the statement: nowadays there is no intellectual in the world whose guts haven't been examined through the exit. If only with a fingernail, or half a finger. The asshole is open to anything, he thinks and laughs, while observing how the color of the sea changes during twilight. And he entertains himself zealously, thinking how much he would've liked to have played trombone in a tropical orchestra, like Willie Colon's, why not, what that would've been like, he says to himself, and laughs and enumerates all the things he didn't do and that in another life, if there is one, he'd be sure to do: sing in the Teatro Petruzzeli in Barí; be the top goal scorer for the Club Atlético Atlanta, and also wear the number nine shirt for the national soccer team; leading man of soap operas; goldsmith in Villa La Angostura willing to attend to tourists and be a playboy and occasional pimp for European millionaires and guilty gringas. Granted none of those beat the line of work Marina came up with, to sew gold buttons once we land on Mars. Or to be the blue Superman cat, as Tomi proposed.

And that very thought changes the course of his reflections because a sudden pang of guilt crushes him like a rock. Not to have been able to save Sarita, who died looking at him without looking at him, her eyes staring out of a hollow statue, is too powerful an accusation. Coming from no one, from the air, the silence of that cadaver was as unyielding and heavy as a tombstone. Bruno Fólner will never know if that blank stillness was appreciation, panic, or indictment.

Perhaps I should have sought refuge in the law instead of running away, he says to himself.

Perhaps I should have just stayed put, if life's going to stick its finger up my ass anyway.

33

"It's going well," he says to himself and takes out a small cigar from the little flowered tin that he'd placed on the table as soon as he got there. He rolls it delicately between his fingers and lights it with a wooden match. He savors the aromatic tobacco and repeats: "It's going well."

But he doesn't know if it's all going well. The fatso from Immigration disturbed him more than anticipated, and his story left him as anxious as teenage girls in bloom when they start to feel their bodies explode.

After twenty years of not smoking, now, with self-imposed and newly forged discipline, he will allow himself to savor a couple small cigars each day. Without paper, small Dutch cigars that he bought on the hill. Or a Montecristo, if I come across one. The same goes for a joint; in Brazil smoking pot is like drinking wine in Mendoza.

This is my first cigar in a decade and a half, so it deserves a little ceremony, ladies and gentlemen, he says to himself, with private solemnity. Then good old Bruno Fólner lights it and inhales with closed eyes, which he opens as he lets out the smoke and looks at the sea.

He feels his heart beat faster and what seems like a slight dizziness. Normal, he tells himself, after not smoking for so long.

That fucking fatso, he thinks next, although he went to the police station that morning and everything was quick and easy. They didn't give him a hard time at all, rather it seemed they were relieved to get the Argentine off their back.

He opens his eyes at the exact moment he sees the maneuvers of a boat with a tall mast and sails unfurled, out on the open bay. It must be Bulão's sailboat, he tells himself, recognizing the cream-colored sails rigged to the foremast and fluttering over the bow. He has yet to learn about ships and sailboats, or to meet Bulão, but he's heard about him. That very night, he'll be coming to see him to have a conversation, because we have here the distinguished Señor Fólner — Jorginho is much more effusive on the phone than in person — who is in need of someone who may provide first-rate service to take him out to sea and sail along the large beaches, and so you will come tonight, Bulãozinho, and the two of you can make arrangements and discuss fees, with a little cachaça on the house to seal the deal, ¿né?

He smiles as he recalls the way the innkeeper handled the matter. Nice guy, he's taken a liking to him. Although it could be dangerous if besides being nice, he's a talker, which in fact he is. But the truth be told, he liked Jorginho and his clan.

He decided to distance himself, all the same, as a precautionary measure, something he started the moment he paid in advance for the third week of lodging.

He opens his Mac and places the Moleskine next to it, and as he exhales a mouthful of smoke, a bit thicker than the last, he remembers Chantal, how Chantal would smoke one Gitanes after another. Those were very intense days, sex and hashish all the time and contemplating the Seine as if it were God the Father. How long ago was that, how many years, thirty? But in Paris, sweet daddy, he says to himself, in the very center of the universe and screwing like rabbits before the world came to an end. Chantal lived in an apartment that was so miniscule it was as if they were fucking inside a wardrobe. But it was Paris.

Oh how he'd love to see Chantal again. See her, of course, the way she used to be, with that body of an adolescent and those firm perky little breasts, panting while she jumped on him as if she were running the two hundred meter hurdles in the Olympics. Granted I'm no longer the man I used to be either, don't be an idiot; this potbelly, these wrinkles, this balding head and gray hair, and this exhaustion can testify to that, he admits, being sensible and sincere. But how wonderful it would be to have a rendezvous of old-timers, making love tenderly and very thoughtfully, with Chantal singing one of Edith Piaf's songs. Perhaps now, with her breasts sagging a bit, but certainly with the same beautiful legs, the same passion she had back then, thirty years ago, that wild little Frenchie. And he smiles and records this fantasy in the Moleskine, transcribing it just the way he thinks it, and then he wonders what his cherished friend Elena must be up to. It's been a while since they saw each other, the last time she was in Mykonos with a husband, who was a policeman and tried to beat her, and on top of that, her teenage daughter had gotten knocked up by a Tunisian who expected to take her away to who knows what kind of Islamic revolution.

Yes, how he'd like to be with Chantal in Paris; what a lovely dream. Of course it's all idle talk, good only for keeping him from writing, because lately, I don't write a thing that's worth a damn, he says to himself, while he waits for Caími to show up with his whisky, and then Bulão.

34.

After striking a deal, the captain leaves; it won't be tomorrow, but the day after, and he'll handle everything, don't worry, *o senhor pode confiar*, trust me.

Then he orders a bountiful seafood salad nestled in a bed of greens, a glass of mineral water, and no more whisky tonight, thank you, two was enough. I'll have a glass of whatever Malbec you have open, thanks.

After dinner, he goes up to his room to read for a while, perhaps the novel he hasn't yet finished, or the thick volume of *Les Misérables* he brought to reread. He always admired Victor Hugo's epic tale, and for years has been planning this rendezvous. And besides, if he can't sleep, perhaps he can write something in the Moleskine or Mac.

But as soon as he enters, and before shutting the door, he senses someone's there. Alarms go off instantly, but then he realizes who it might be and proceeds with caution, first by not turning on the light. The radiance of the Atlantic evening enters the wide-open window, and Bruno Fólner stares, motionless, into the half-light, unable to confirm if what he's seeing is real; if it's happening or if he's dreaming.

He moves toward her without saying her name, without a word, his eyes piercing the shadows, until he makes out the silhouette of that white figure outlined against the window. Never in his life has he seen anything like that imprinted on his eyes. He knows that beneath the white dress, she's naked, completely breathtaking, and clearly for him, he thinks. He can't believe what's happening, because if it's truly happening, he doesn't need to pinch himself. Or should he? He feels overwhelmed. What's real and what's imagined blend together once again, more than ever, and he doesn't have a better idea than to reach his hand out to turn on the lamp on the nightstand, an action she halts with a barely audible voice, no, don't do that. Then, not knowing what to do, he takes off his canvas shoes and undresses slowly, while keeping his eyes glued to that figure defined by the exterior light, who in turn, abandons the window, and undresses as well, before sitting down on the edge of the bed. She's lifted her dress over her shoulders and her nakedness is voluptuous and vast, as if it encompassed the entire world. A ray of moonlight casts shimmering flecks on the dark skin of her legs. Both now naked, Bruno feels ugly, old, and ridiculous, albeit touched by the gods, and thinks none of this makes sense, and that's a good thing, there are no explanations, it's just what it is, and this is what it is, and he looks and admires her feet, large and shining like bronze in that filtered light.

At that point, he doesn't know what to do, and leaves it up to her, and she kneels down and leans over him and kisses his mouth gently. It's been a million years since Bruno Fólner felt what he's feeling now, an unexpected warmth coursing through him from head to toe. Perhaps because it was only a few days ago that he was born, and the decades he lived as G.R. no longer matter. Then she kisses him sweetly on the neck, on one shoulder, on the nipples, sliding over his exposed belly and, like someone who comes to the end of a road, she traps the bird between her lips and caresses it with her tongue, sucking it like a baby who falls asleep with the bottle in her mouth.

Many times he's dreamed about making love this way, being loved this way: hands and mouth deployed as instruments of pleasure, not as simple body parts but as matter slipping into a hollow. It took me four decades that seemed like four centuries to find it, he says to himself with diminishing sorrow, and extends his hand and strokes her, barely touches her, caresses her skin and feels, little by little, a delectable euphoria, as he realizes that indeed it's possible to make love with the entire body, and that in order to burrow into that beloved cavern, all that's needed is the blessing of desire, the mutual consent of the body for one to make love with elbows, ankles, neck, liver, wrists, pituitary gland, and of course the nose, ears, and yes, all of them symbolic paths leading to the brain. This is what it means to love with the entire body, convert hearing, what is said and understood, into substance.

Especially with the tongue, his tongue that now kisses softly the contours of Rejane's secret chamber, which spreads open like a butterfly and allows him to do as he wishes and he does: he explores her kiss by kiss, first wetting her thighs and the base of her buttocks, and then kissing the vulva as one would kiss a magnificent sacred chalice, sipping the emerging juices, an elixir that springs forth as if responding to the siege of desire. With his tongue he loves her, makes love to her, penetrates her as deeply as possible, stirs and excites her, guiding her with boldness and soothing her, calming her, and she surrenders completely, and also accepts his bidding, his rule, as she lets herself go with a restrained shout, with a moan that finally explodes, gushing in quivering waves. Rejane overflows and suddenly pees, actually pees, no metaphor, a long hot stream spills out of her and floods the bed, leaving both of them wet and free like Paris on the day of liberation, like the little *Casa de Tucumán*, the birthplace of independence two hundred years ago, like the eyes of Sarita while he, G. R., now Bruno Fólner, was killing her, mercifully but illegally. Everything comes together in this new flooded valley in which he becomes erect and spreads her open, looking at her for an instant before penetrating her deeply and with a force he didn't know he possessed, and he begins entering and leaving that welcoming body, that fluid body that desires and loves and possesses as if in the midst of a final widespread mass destruction.

Perhaps the essence of love lies in this miracle, thinks Bruno Fólner afterward, lying exhausted next to Rejane, in silence, with lights and shadows flickering up and down the sheets. Paraphrasing Juan Gelman I could say now, he whispers to himself, that from this moment, I can leave my eyes deep inside this woman and wouldn't mind being blind.

Say it again, she asks. You talk so pretty, say it again. And he repeats it his way, not word by word, but with a flourish, and adds that in exchange for this one night, I'd forget my entire life, renounce it until there's nothing left but silence and the muted clamor of millions of birds.

Rejane smiles, her eyes glistening with the sea, as she takes her leave with grace and disappears.

Bruno Fólner knows that some beings can't live without the sea.

35.

He stays in his room in the morning. He had a dream that he missed the plane in Fortaleza, and they boarded him on one headed for Tallinn, where was Tallinn? Just an invention, that city, completely unknown. He complained to the stewardesses, who told him if he didn't like it, he could get off, and they laughed like taunting little devils and their giggles grew louder and louder, until the shrillness pierced his ears like a chorus of manufactured mermaids screeching in his head, and then he woke up, confused, his heart racing. He went to the bathroom, urinated, and took two Losartan potassium pills. My blood pressure must be through the roof, damn it, he says to himself and decides to stay in bed.

That's what he did, and that's where he is, lying in the softly lit dimness of an ocean view room.

Until he hears someone knocking very softly at the door, and he goes and opens it and there she is again. A bit fleshier, gorgeous, all aglow in bright white, barefoot and with a shawl over her shoulders.

He steps aside and she enters like a breeze penetrating an abandoned house.

"Do you always do this?"

"I don't do anything. And don't ask questions," she says, using the familiar form in Portuguese, and she stands in the middle of the room, looking around with childish curiosity.

"Jorginho should announce you."

She ignores the comment and asks for music, *por favor*. Bruno turns on the small radio recorder on the desk, and the lovely, mournful voice of Cristina Branco can be heard singing "*Navio triste*." Rejane sings along in a soft voice, swaying a bit. Bruno goes over to her and moves his hips slightly as well. He dances with her, although they don't touch each other. Their bodies move harmoniously, without contact, until the voice fades out, and the two of them, now facing each other, stop short of embracing and simply stroke each other's arms with a light and gentle touch. Then she caresses his face, running two fingers over it delicately. Her hand smells of lavender, of recently applied lotion, and Bruno feels a tingle as her fingers glide tenderly over his weathered skin, and he keeps his eyes closed, fearful that such a beautiful thing will come to an end, what seems to be a spell, and perhaps truly is.

Then Rejane tells him about the morning, this morning, or perhaps another one. She was in the motor boat that Zé María, the guide and fishmonger, rents out to tourists. Once again nothing, she says, going out and coming back to no avail. Empty-handed. Desperate. And the same thing, one day after another, and the days go by, she says, and a week, then two and three, and months and years. And she goes into the sea and swims, and nothing. She swims in all directions, swims asking the ocean about Marco, and nothing, swims and swims turning into a mermaid, ghost, white specter, lady of the waterfront and beach, weary image of despair.

No poem could ever tell this tale, she says. Marco never appeared again and I went with him, she adds. End of story.

Bruno Fólner understands that that woman is pure pain, a burning ember.

36.

An outing at sea, alone with Bulão. He's seated on the bow, wearing a life-jacket, his face battered by the wind, which seems to etch the seascape on his skin. The boat is ten meters long, with an outboard motor and an awning in the middle that functions as a tent to cover the plank, used as a table, beneath which are some bottles secured in a box stowed in the center next to a cooler, undoubtedly, full of ice and beers.

The boat rocks, and he no longer watches Bulão, who's a fairly intelligent guy and also as sensitive and elusive as a sea bass. The first time he saw him, he was reminded of Gordo Núñez. Failure is certain for guys like them, especially if they risk offering their opinion. Luckily, this guy isn't a talker. Discretion is his key to survival. And he knows how to maneuver the small boat, as Jorginho had guaranteed.

Bruno Fólner can't help but think about another boat trip, the last one he remembers, twenty some years ago, in Honolulu. It was on a typical Hawaiian catamaran with four couples on board. A French couple, and the rest gringos, Sarita and him. She was as beautiful as always, and above all, happy. She was wearing some kind of white sun hat, tied under her chin, and she smiled the entire time, like someone who's guaranteed eternal happiness. She was an adorable woman, and his duty was to take photos of her with the sea and sun and beach in the picture. At times, happiness is so simple it goes unnoticed. They sailed to a kind of fiord, with crags pierced by the rhythmic motion of the sea going in and out, and the little boat nearly crashed and had to turn around there, and that was what made the experience so unforgettable.

Now he's beginning to have doubts: didn't they also go sailing in Acapulco, a vacation they took with the Alcántaras, Ricky and Laura, and it was a real drag because they argued the whole time? That is, the Alcántaras, he thinks now, like cats and dogs. I never understood why Sarita liked them so much.

Sarita, his victim whether he recognizes it or not, comes and goes, like the sea.

Like spirits, when they're alive.

Like regrets, which never let up. They come and go, like the sea.

They dock on one side of the pier, in the little marina, surrounded by rocks.

"*Obrigado*, Bulão," lovely cruise.

And he walks down the boardwalk toward the inn.

37.

After that extraordinary night, some mornings he wakes up and checks to see if he's alone. It was all a dream, evidently. Rejane isn't here, she doesn't exist, he thinks as the dawn light filters through the heavy curtains. And yet he feels — yes, he has a feeling — that her scent lingers on the sheets and in the air, but without Rejane.

Pure fantasy on your part, Fólner. Blunt, skeptical, and yet, amazed because he remembers everything so vividly.

He's dreamed that it's Sunday, early in the afternoon, and she enters.

"You have any *yerba mate* here?"

Bruno nods his head toward the bathroom.

"There's a gourd by the sink and the thermos still has hot water."

She goes into the bathroom and comes out with both hands full.

"What are you writing?" she asks while setting the thermos on the table and swirling the metal straw in the gourd, staring at him all the while.

"I just finished a story. It didn't have an ending, but at this very moment, you're giving me one."

"What a lie!" she says with a delightful shriek of laughter: "Lying Argentine."

Then he gets up, goes to the bathroom, rubs his eyes, splashes water on his face, and looks at himself in the mirror. He sees a completely wrinkled face, his beard and the few hairs on his head are definitely white and disheveled, as if they'd been through a windstorm. He remembers how he loved those mornings when Sarita used to tell him that after making love and getting a good night's rest, his wrinkles disappeared, making him look ten years younger. He cracks a smile, but it seems sad, a woefully mournful, stupid smile that some idiot fugitive sketched on the mirror. He turns and goes back to the bedroom.

The window is open now. He doesn't remember having opened it, but the two panes look out on the luminous morning. He scouts the boardwalk to see if she's walking along it, surveying all the way to the pier and above, to the top of the hill, trying to scrutinize everything as if he had binoculars. The end result is nothing, nothing, of course. Reluctantly, he has to admit his eyesight is also failing him. For the most part, he sees well with glasses, but with the passing years comes unrelenting fatigue, and at times his vision gets cloudy. Like now. Something's out of focus, rays of light overlap, and he has to make minor adjustments to see clearly. And even then he has trouble, especially when the light is so bright. And also when night begins to fall and he feels the weariness in his open eyes. He must be getting those damned cataracts; inevitable for a guy who's depended on his eyes his whole life, to end up with some visual deterioration. Then he looks toward the water to see if she's out there, swimming in another void, and then closes his eyes and squeezes his eyelids tight like someone who becomes enraged before the hopeless presence of God.

He closes the window and puts on a pair of pants, a clean shirt, and opens the door and goes down to the dining room.

Upon entering, he greets Dona Amalia, and then goes over to Jorginho and asks him if he saw her leave and at what time.

Jorginho looks him square in the eye, with his eagle eyes, and it's as if both pierce the pupils of the other.

Bruno Fólner goes over to the public computer and reads the newspapers at random, with a cup of coffee at his side. In a site from the Chaco, he reads this sentence, written by some anonymous fool, in reference to a local news story: ". . . those who commit murder and flee, convinced perhaps of their own false mercy." He reads it two times. Three. He feels uncomfortable in the chair. Bullshit, that comment. It's just the shit they publish in newspapers these days. Websites are full of imbeciles, resentful sons of bitches.

After finishing his coffee, he feels even more anxious. And something very insidious is alarming and agitating him. He's not sure what, but he plays with the alliteration. The play on words distracts him for a few moments, until he recognizes something familiar off in the distance, out front, across the avenue and on the boardwalk, about one hundred fifty meters, in the direction of the hill. He jumps instantly when he recognizes that the obese figure, who apparently just happens to be there, is none other than that son of a bitch pig with yellow teeth.

38.

"What are you writing?" she asks, appearing out of the blue. "You always have a worried look on your face, a very intense, focused look."

Bruno lifts his head and looks at her, raising his eyebrows.

Suddenly, as if catapulted, he stands up like a coward. He can't hold her gaze or return her smile, or maintain a conversation with that woman, who suddenly now represents something that terrorizes him.

Panic sets in. He takes a few steps, quickly and decisively like a cockroach, and with an unusual nimbleness for his age. He peers out on the porch that faces the boardwalk, and takes a deep breath of ocean air. Then he heads for the restaurant's bathroom and shuts himself inside, where the lightbulb has burned out and the light entering the window creates a kind of filtered clarity. That detail makes him think that perhaps he doesn't have much more time, that he's inundated with what he figures is the typical guilt of an assassin on the run, and on top of that, he asks himself, not much time for what, and doesn't know how to put his finger on it.

He returns and observes the slow unsteady gait of a little lame girl on the beach. She's very young, still a child, and evokes a vague memory of a Czech family he met years ago, who still live on a very pretty farm, on the border between Salta and Formosa. The Bakucz family grows vegetables and keeps goats in a corral and chickens in a coop, and have an enormous fig tree in the back. Their only daughter was born with a defect in one leg, which is shorter than the other. She walks leaning to one side and kind of on tiptoes because the right leg ends in a stub and has no toes. She's identical to the girl who always walks along the beach.

"Waldira," Rejane has said to him. "She's my friend and her name is Waldira. She's missing part of her foot, but she makes up for it with her heart. Haven't you heard her singing?"

Bruno shakes his head no.

"Well then you haven't heard the angels of the sea."

They're face to face and looking into each other's eyes, and he thinks how much he'd like to kiss her. She's by far the most attractive woman he's ever met in his life. She must be close to fifty and is still so beautiful; hard to imagine what she must have been like in her twenties. Dark-skinned women seem to celebrate the kilos that add up over the years. And that wide mouth and full lips entice me more than a plateful of crabs. He smiles thinking about it. But he doesn't make a move; he's lost the nerve he once had. It's better to wait. And he waits, until she says, they say you came here to escape.

"What?" he asks, uneasy, looking quickly and anxiously toward the door, the window, and outside. He recognizes his panic.

"People talk, speculate . . . Everything comes to an end."

Bruno Fólner composes himself. He wants that visit to end, that is, if it is a visit, so he can calm himself down.

In addition to her mouth, he looks at her feet. He really likes that woman, but fear takes over, as intense as a chili habanero ten seconds after you bite into it.

"You're an interesting man, Bruno."

"How would you know that?"

"A person's not interesting if he doesn't have stories to forget."

"Says who?"

She remains silent and looks beyond the sea, like someone who detects rain on the horizon.

"I don't know who you are either, Rejane."

"I'm the past, nothing more."

Bruno imagines drawing near, but she steps back. Their bodies seem to regain their independence. His mouth feels dry, his nose stuffed up. The way he used to feel after making love, exhausted, drained, complete.

Those were other times, he says to himself without nostalgia, and without saying a word. That must be why happiness has no place in literature:

because only behind each sin is there a story that deserves to be told. Dante's fame is based on *Hell*, not *Paradise*. Happy people have photo albums. And nowadays Facebook, Instagram, YouTube.

Weary, he collapses into a deck chair. He knows he's being rude for no reason, but he doesn't care. The red flags have him on edge.

39.

People believe, like they believe many things, as do you yourself, that at sixty-five, a man is finished. He thinks about Onetti's story, "Welcome, Bob": "You're a grown man, that's to say washed-up, like all men your age, unless they're exceptional." He smiles. But not nowadays, when it seems the old aren't old and you can have dreams and fantasies at any age. They've published studies, and I've read about it in tons of articles, and besides, if you want to know the truth, love is never a closed door, and who doesn't wish for utopia. As for me, desire still makes me catch my breath, and I'm not ashamed of my naked body, or not totally. My wrinkles and white hair have stories to tell that I won't deny. I'm a sex-agenarian, he concludes smiling and approving of himself in the mirror, before going down for breakfast. He plans to walk for a couple hours, past the town, heading south.

This exile, he thinks, while he sits with his first steaming cup of coffee beneath his nose, this kind of escape from my own life, this new migrant condition, which surely will be permanent, might actually provide material or inspiration for the new novel I've been dreaming about. One that's been left stranded like a beached whale.

He'd thought about calling it *The Mendoza Lovers*, but it's a lousy title. *The Days that Never Dawn Again* would be better. Or *Dark Night on the Mountain*. Or *Before the Snow Falls*. Those are good. Of course, it's not even started; for now it's just an idea, four words to kick it off, powerful and disturbing, but not enough, and a ton of crap scribbled in the Moleskine.

The problem is I don't know how to get over this paralysis, this compulsion of thinking and feeling like a fugitive who's lying low and doesn't know if the hounds are on his trail. But the Immigration Pig is an indication that perhaps I'm not reading this correctly. Watch out, Fólner. Of course, I don't know what the hell to do. Move on, but where to? And how not to leave a trail? And besides, I like it here. I have no way of knowing if some son of a bitch in the Chaco is looking into the case and on my trail. When it comes to the cops, you can never be sure.

If I were a drug lord or dangerous criminal, Interpol would be after me, and they'd put wanted posters everywhere. But I'm just a poor sucker, so I might get away with it.

Or it'll be easier to take me down. Who knows?

Yes, more coffee, thank you Laurinha. And pineapple juice too, of course.

All my life I've been an avid reader of detective novels, but that's not helping me figure things out now. I don't recall a situation like this one, and can't find advice for myself.

Perhaps everything's already been said, and in a superb way. There's been nothing original since Homer and Cervantes. It's just that originality doesn't exist. Not the story within a story, which is older than the love for a mother. Nor the novel within the novel, which Cervantes already did. You can revisit tales, stories and novels you wrote, and recall how you dealt with death, betrayal, vengeance, and pain, in each case. But that's not enough when you're faced with something concrete, that you can touch, that's not intellectual. The death of Sarita, for example, is sticky and clings to me. It's like a trickle of molasses that oozes from a leaky gutter. The gutter is screwed to a beam in the ceiling of the mind, let's say, and the drops of sugar land on you while you're sleeping. And you wake up all sticky, sickly-sweet, and in a panic because ants are crawling all over you.

Dona Amalia's fresh pineapple juice is so delicious. It's such a treat, thank you my dear. No thank you, nothing else, *tudo bem*.

I feel like I'm getting depressed, he says to himself as he rubs the palms of his hands over his face. The only thing I ever wanted to do was tell a good story. Maybe rewrite the one about *El Perro Fernando*, iconic symbol of Resistencia's intellectual void. Or that older one, about the two drunks who hunted ducks from a plane. No, not even that one.

Then he remembers that Brazil was actually the destination for his first trips as a writer. Once in a provincial book fair in Caxias do Sul, I had a blast, drinking beer like crazy. And another time, I went to a conference at a university in Passo Fundo, where it snowed all night long. It was the most unexpected and absurd thing in the world: snow in Brazil, what the fuck, he thought as he looked out his hotel window and watched the snowflakes fall. From there, he remembered way back, to a forum organized by UNESCO, when Brasilia was still a fledgling little town, and he discovered a stray scorpion in his bed, alive and deadly, and as threatening as Arreola's tarantula.

We're not free, he says to the mirror. Never. And much less with the hounds closing in.

But it's possible they'll never find you and nothing will happen, Fólner, so go ahead, keep wasting time while you try to rid yourself of the guilt you feel. No one's coming for you, and it will all be forgotten, okay? That's it. Who cares if you killed your wife, if you did it out of mercy and after a decent life, completely normal, by all appearances, like anyone else's? Your sudden disappearance from the Argentine cultural scene hasn't left an irreparable hole, or stirred up any chitchat or commotion. Perhaps some minor local repercussion, some turmoil in town, and a photo in the "Mirador," the Sunday supplement to the *El Sol del Chaco*. Pure shit. Your getaway and presumed death might even result in a slight increase in sales of your four novels, not for their literary merit, but out of that old morbid public fascination.

That's how it is, Fólner, he tells himself. And he begins to feel miserable, empty.

Beautiful morning, he says to himself later, as he feels the wind tousling the few hairs he had carefully combed when he got up. He looks in the mirror and puts those last stray hairs in place, beholding his baldness. Only now does he notice he's much balder than when he left the hospital. And to think of the full head of hair he used to have, shit, not only was it abundant, thick, and strong, but at times, it would shine as if his brilliant ideas and thoughts added volume and style. Not this poor, gray, lackluster hair. Like me.

He finishes his third cup of coffee, after the pineapple juice, and stays there looking at the horizon, feeling like an empty seashell.

40.

When he saw her the first time in his room, he wondered if she could be a hooker. He felt stupid immediately, but couldn't help but wonder. Insecurity, he said to himself, after so many years. Who'd be interested in me at this stage of the game?

She has just told him, softly and candidly, that he can't make demands, that he shouldn't fear or question anything, or insist, or have expectations. The waves come and go, she says, thanks to the sea.

Bruno Fólner doesn't understand what's happening, but the mounting confusion paralyzes him. Panic spreads inside him, like when a plane crashes or a ship sinks. All is sound without fury, high alert, helplessness.

He looks at her in the dim light and wonders if that gorgeous captivating woman, who doesn't seem to be of this world, could be real. As if dreaming, he contemplates her tall robust body, her legs, firm as wood, and that Mona Lisa hint of a smile, slight and enigmatic. She bears the mark of life's experiences and maternities that have enlarged her breasts. Bruno Fólner asks himself if she could be a figment of his imagination to assuage his guilt, the remorse that pursues him. Because he can't stop thinking about Sarita and the kids, who are no longer his, except in his own paternal thoughts. Or those of an ex-father, he should say. He corrects himself and becomes irritated. He no longer knows if his children will acknowledge him.

He returns to the serene figure he sees there, in the shadows. Observing her in the complicit stillness of the room ignites a distant, unusual hint of desire, a tingling between his legs he hasn't felt for quite some time. For months, perhaps years. Even before Sarita got sick, they no longer initiated passionate moves in their house in Resistencia. And his sex, one-time loyal companion, remains lethargic, as if lost in a long sleep.

"Look at the sea with me," she asks. He goes over to her, but doesn't embrace her. There are no kisses or caresses, only an intimacy, more fraternal than ardent, as if charged with the nostalgia of ancient passions.

There comes a time when you no longer know how to approach the queen, he thinks now. It's not that you feel like a king, but the queen doesn't always make the move one expects, and the game goes to hell. Better a pair of rooks. Or not, who knows. Delay and stall. The pawns look at the field without understanding, with blind eyes, open but lost, trying to restrain the poor king who falters, checked by the opposing bishops who control the diagonals. Totally screwed. Move to any square, and you'll get beat.

He hesitates, but somehow they make love, with less intensity than tenderness, with caresses that seem endless in the initial exploration of their skin. Perhaps at one moment, cautious and patient, they will unleash a whirlwind of desire. But that doesn't happen now, when they lie down, and one mounts the other, who then takes a turn on top. And they begin again, and perhaps later, he will enter her gently, but at this moment, he can't hold back that searing wail rising from his soul, and he breaks down and cries with unrestrained grief.

She senses that the battle-scarred body on top of her is moving to an unanticipated and unusual rhythm, and even shedding tears that trickle between her breasts. Seconds later, he breaks down and weeps openly, brokenhearted, in deep full-fledged pain.

"¡Caralho!" she murmurs in Portuguese, as if to herself. "Many things have happened to me in this life, but never has an old man cried on my tits."

The two laugh and Bruno Fólner lifts his head and looks at her with his weepy eyes that seem to have been hammered deeply into a flushed face, which reflects in that instant hundreds of years.

"You should see yourself," she says, "you look like an octopus tossed out in the sun."

Bruno Fólner likes that image, but it repulses him at the same time, and he wonders if perhaps everything had been just a dream. It could be, he tells himself, and maybe it should be. Only the intricate logic of a dream would explain that behavior in a woman who everyone believes and says comes from the sea, and is not real.

41.

Sarita. One memory, one thought about Sarita, even if it's fiction. That's what's needed, if only to defy the persistence of oblivion. Guilt is, like her, a bolt of lightning that never strikes.

What more to say?

That she was a warm scarf in the winter, a hushed softness sometimes, a whirlwind of rage and resentment many others.

How I liked it when she'd curse Rousseau. She was so amusing. She'd become a feminist in her later years, and I felt so proud watching her conduct herself with confidence, integrity, autonomy. I loved to see how other women in town admired and envied her. Although there was something about her that made her distant, often unsociable, as if her nerves were on edge. Although that was part of her contradictory charm, it bothered me. I asked her many times, in the beginning, what that was all about, how was I letting her down. But she'd hold my hand and tell me sweetly it was nothing, that everything with me was fine, that I shouldn't pay attention to her.

It was an unforgettable evening, in Paso de la Patria, breezy and without mosquitos, when after a stupid but intense argument, Sarita confessed to me, that was the verb, that many years before, at the university, a classmate who was her boyfriend, the son of parents from Tucumán who were biochemists, or something like that, had hurt her one night, and because she resisted, he went crazy and hurt her even more, a lot more.

She was studying to get into Medical School and was still a virgin, and above all naive and dumb, she said tensing up, and that son of a bitch who used to feel her up all over when they kissed in alcoves or corners, in the plaza or at school, hurt her so much, she thought she'd never be able to let down her guard.

She said the problem had nothing to do with me, but it was still a problem.

Please, understand me.

And I, who was G.R. back then and loved her to death, opted to remain silent at first, but later insisted on knowing what had happened. Something terrible must have happened to you that makes you so aloof, I realize that, I'd tell her, so if you don't want to tell me, don't tell me, but I know something's wrong and it's going to continue doing us harm if you keep it to yourself.

And yet Sarita remained silent for years. She'd cry and recover and cry again an endless number of times, and I started to piece things together from different conversations. He was a jealous and possessive guy who became more and more insistent each time she resisted giving in to him. Sarita's parents were very liberal for the times, but not oblivious, and they'd warned her about the boyfriend, who was a nice kid, talkative, charming and a good dancer, but too obsessed, you could see that from a mile away, according to her old man. But she didn't listen, or was confused, or whatever, and stayed with him, genuinely blind, until one night, after returning from a school party, he raped her in the back seat of a friend's car. He hurt her terribly when he penetrated her, pounded her with his fists to subdue her but then felt impotent, which made things worse because he became even more enraged. Sarita choked up when she recalled how that son of a bitch punched her face and breasts, completely out of control, and kicked her in the crotch, and each time she tried to scream for help, he became more and more brutal. It was all so horrible, and the guy was so monstrous that he got out of the car and left her crying, but a few minutes later, after pissing on a tree, he returned to end the torture with a threat: tomorrow you'll say you fell down the stairs, or else things will get even worse for you.

Luckily she didn't get pregnant, and after that, with the help of my in-laws, who are so kind, Sara was able to recover, although those wounds last forever. She could never stop being elusive, wary, reluctant to surrender. Without knowing all this, I loved her the way she was, but it was hard to endure. And only much later, after the kids and many years, was she able to loosen up little by little and find happiness again. Only recently, in her forties, when she devoured books on the feminine condition and traditional gender roles, and read Jean-Jacque Rousseau, cursing him from head to toe, did she become the superbly marvelous woman I loved so much. Until that one afternoon when she got sick and the agony of her physical deterioration began.

I don't know why I'm remembering all this now. Perhaps because Hugo is as French as Rousseau, although less of an asshole. Going back from the nineteenth to the eighteenth century, when Rousseau instituted the feminine role of subordination that would later become canonic: the passive and weak guardian of the home, devotee to her husband, kind-hearted and all the rest. An image that prevailed for two centuries, and is only being shattered now, Sarita would proclaim, enough of subjugation and accepting the unacceptable.

That also screwed my gender and my generation, thinks Bruno Fólner with sorrow, as he pours more wine into his glass.

Sarita was also a pillar. A rock to cling to in rough water, someone who shed private tears, but offered a firm hand and tender look whenever someone stumbled.

As precious as gold.

42.

Fólner, you've got it together. Cool, calm, and collected, Fólner, and in your sixties. I don't know how long it'll last, but it's a fantastic feeling.

So strange to feel like this. But it helps to keep regrets at bay, not just the guilt over Sarita, but also over the kids.

Because I left them alone, in every sense. I killed their old lady, but also their father. They'll never see me again, and for them, that's the same as if I'd died. Damn it, I didn't think that through.

Surely they hate me now, and they'd reject me if they saw me, because it was a multiple homicide.

Shit, that sound's awful, brutal. But that's what it was.

It's over, hell, I don't want to think about that.

Now there's another guy: Bruno Fólner. This old codger who welcomes each new day and is capable of having an intense night of sex and sleeping soundly like a teenager afterwards. Without a clear conscience, but able to ward off that recurring ant dream he's had since he was a boy.

I narrated that dream in a novel, it doesn't matter which, at this stage of the game accuracy is futile. Even though you might feel like you have it together, changing the subject is always a good tactic. Ideal for not thinking about the family, rather my ex-family, the family I lost, or killed, raffled off, wiped out, what the hell.

It's a very old dream, your typical adolescent nightmare. He's a beautiful blooming plant or bush that's attacked systematically by thousands of ants scurrying up and down. He shudders and the ants fall off, but others always rally to carry out the task. Of course, after so much shaking and jumping, he grows weary. But they continue, relentless, infinite, as they hack away at him, eat him, carry him off, reduced to bits of leaves and branches they ravage slowly, imperiously, without yielding, while he screams in pain from their stinging bites. Desperation takes over, and he tries again to shake them loose, he no longer has the strength, and the ants overcome him. And that's when he remembers that he's had that nightmare other times and he knows how it ends, or believes he knows, and then he wakes up, sweaty and exhausted, with anxiety that lasts the whole fucking day.

But I still have it together. Even at my age.

What the fuck. I'm itching all over. Ants are devouring me, I'm just a cadaver, that's all I am. A dead man who walks because he doesn't know he's dead.

The encounter with Rejane, if it was an encounter, was also a test, a personal one, just for me, and I passed. One hour sawing away, back and forth, and I didn't wear out, although in the end, I crashed like a dead man, exhausted, pulverized. And I slept like a corpse. Expired, extinguished, wiped out.

But during that hour of thrusting and thrusting, I was a bull. Astonishing, unusual virility for a sex-agenerian. Bada bing, bada bang.

Fantastic feeling, no fucking way. There's no going back. There's no forgiveness. Yes, you're cool, but screwed. You couldn't make a move even with a crane up your ass.

43.

Smoldering but silent, Rejane seems to express herself, above all, through concentrated breathing, mute pleasure, and passion as deep as a coal mine. Bruno Fólner adores her silence, knowing it's blind bliss seeking refuge behind closed eyes. Now, while the raucous sea churns outside, portending a storm, he longs to hear her moan. That restrained expression, closed tight as a clam, resonates in that woman of seasoned beauty, with dark eyelids, fringed by lashes thick as a brush. Bruno Fólner admires her supple curves, which remind him of those miniature Renaissance scenes that grace porcelain tea cups and plates, and asks himself if he deserves this prize, and a prize for what, and why.

I deserve nothing but condemnation. From everyone, but especially my children. I didn't think it through, that's for certain. Not before and not now. I would've told them, sworn to them that I loved them with all my heart and soul, and that what I did was an act of love, a righteous act of love so their mother wouldn't suffer any longer. I would've explained and sworn that we'd made a pact when we got married, promising to help the other, whichever was the first to suffer the dreadful ravages of cancer, Alzheimer's, or a stroke that leaves you worse off than a puppet. I would've sworn that we swore to each other, but they would've looked at me in horror. I turned them into orphans, of Sara and me too. There's no remedy for this. There's no turning back, that's for certain, there's no going back.

He holds his head in his hands with his elbows on the tablecloth, and senses a deluge of tears welling up, and then suddenly stands up and leaves the room.

He needs fresh air and there's more than enough of that in Praia Macacos.

44.

That night, in the wee hours, after the sea had soothed its fury and suspended its threat, the voice of Sarita awakens him.

He knows immediately he's having a nightmare; he knows, because
it isn't the first time she's called out to him from the darkness. That's why he
keeps his eyes closed and thinks about death, although, strangely enough,
not Sarita's. What he remembers now is the day he returned to Resistencia,
after being gone ten years, and Norma, his older sister, suggested they go to
the cemetery. Their parents were there, in two niches, side by side, in the
third row of the fifteenth section. The pavilion was long and cold, even
though it was more than one hundred degrees on the streets of the city.
There were very few mourners in the galleries; just two old people standing
before a niche on a corner, and about twenty meters to the right, a woman
cleaning bronze plaques with a rag.

He walked with Norma down a very long passageway, almost three
blocks, and along a grid of niches in the great wall that seemed to have been
designed by an architect obsessed with symmetry. The yellowish-white color
of the marble stones, engraved with names and dates, helped transform that
extensive checkerboard into a kind of mortuary record in which confusion
reigned over order.

He was impressed by Norma's confidence. Evidently, she knew the
place by heart. Without hesitating, and as if she'd counted the niches from

the corner to keep track, she stopped at one spot and pointed toward the third row, a little above their heads. He did nothing more than step back from the wall, and stand there in silence, asking himself how it was possible for someone to believe that this cold, multitudinous string of marble and bronze could represent something truly personal for someone. Let alone sacred. Actually, he didn't feel a thing, so he just stood there, a few steps behind his sister, watching her scrub the plaques with a rag soaked in Brasso, the brand of cleanser used back then for polishing brass, an action which reminded him of the inn's daily routine of washing plates and silverware after lunch.

He looked at his sister, the way you'd gaze at the *pampa* from a train, taking it all in but focusing on nothing in particular. When she finished and stepped back a bit, as if to evaluate her work from a proper perspective, he admitted to himself that all he really wanted to do was rest with his back against the opposite wall. So he squatted first and then sat down on the floor. And like a child, with legs crossed, he remained silent, watching Norma pray before the two plaques, engraved with the names of their parents, and shining once more. Suddenly, it all seemed sadly familiar. He doesn't remember now if he cried, or just wandered off.

He stares at the empty bed from top to bottom, props himself up on his elbows and looks out at the sea, still black as the night. What's the meaning behind that voice of Sara's, a kind of summons that interrupted his sleep?

He considers several responses, none convincing, until finally falling asleep just before dawn.

45.

"A story, tell me a story, after all, you're a writer," Rejane requests. With her face to the waves, her black hair sways in the wind.

Bruno Fólner has vanquished once again the temptation to check his email. Although he's neglected all his accounts, he could look at them, if only to confirm the silence. Or read complaints.

But no, he couldn't bear it. He doesn't want to read reproaches, accusations from children or relatives. Or from friends.

There is no story, Rejane, nor does it matter if we exist, he wanted to say to her, it doesn't matter if we're pure fantasy, imagination, or merely an interlude, lapsed time. It doesn't matter if old age hounds you like the Devil, even if now, in this very instant, I could be a bull, a cyclops, a centennial *quebracho* tree. But he chides himself for not knowing how to say it. He doesn't speak, and senses that his silence is atrocious. Fólner, you're a fool, an idiot, a disaster. Total fake. And a multiple assassin because you didn't just kill Sara Grinberg.

Nor could he bear the silence, the indifference.

But this is death, and I'm also dead. The one I used to be died.

He's sitting on the edge of the boardwalk, a couple meters away from her. He'd be better off thinking about the novel that no longer seems possible, he tells himself, or about a short story he knows he's not going to write either. His new theory is that the deluge of ideas for short stories is infinite, and therefore unlimited, and so it's useless to attempt to write all of them.

And besides, this particular story is impossible to write because it's the true account of the tragedy of Luchi, his other sister, who exists only in some old photograph taken decades ago, which he didn't bring with him to Brazil, of course. The fugitive doesn't leave a trail, nor does he keep photos, no way.

Luchi's story is very sad, and he knows he'll never write it because he carries it with him like a scar that will never ever heal. They disappeared her when she was very young, and the passing years don't ease the pain or the nostalgia. The tragedy of the country swallowed her up, like the seas and misfortunes vanished the voyagers of the Odyssey.

Only once did he manage to sketch out a kind of draft, soon after he arrived, the only time he stepped foot in Zé Antonio's bar. That night he drank like a fish, pursued by guilt and the vacant accusatory eyes of Sarita that still seemed to stare at him. Right off the bat, he ordered three *caipirinhas* over ice, which blurred his vision and fried his brain, and from that point on, he began to hear a buzzing like a bee trapped in a glass bottle. From what he could remember later, he told Zé Antonio something about Luchi's story, which he immediately considered an error in judgement because, as he later learned, Zé Antonio was one of those maniacal storytellers who believes everything he hears and then reinvents and repeats it, deceiving himself and swallowing his own lies, becoming ensnared in his own traps. What's more, Zé Antonio is a mean drunk, nothing like Bellow's delightful Hattie, rather a rotten Latin American boozer. Had he been a literary character, he'd have spent a lifetime exchanging blows with God and the Virgin Mary herself. A bad-mouthed troublemaker, like one of Bukowski's characters, capable of telling his friends that his brothers screw their sisters-in-law, or that they're crooked bastards, and the next day he can't remember a thing, not even when the insults lead to punches and chairs being hurled. And if by chance he remembers something, it's vague and confusing, and he thinks he can fix everything with weak excuses. And sometimes he does. Some people are like that.

"You'd be better off picking up one of my books and reading it, darling, if you feel like it. Two have been translated to Portuguese."

Rejane continues facing the sea, and then suddenly begins to walk calmly along the beach, an indication to Bruno that she wishes to be alone.

He returns to the hotel, remembering, at the same time, Sarita's dead eyes and Luchi's desperate scream when they abducted her. The weeping and helplessness of everyone in the house that night, more than thirty years ago, also blends in with the predictable brokenhearted sobs of Nico, Tomi and Marina at Sarita's funeral, which he prefers not to imagine.

Piercing and overbearing, he feels a buzzing in his head that reminds him of the trapped bees from Zé Antonio's *caipirinhas*. He closes his eyes and recites: "There are anguishes in dreams, more real than those life deals us; there are sensations felt only by imagining them, more ours than life itself. Hovering over the soul, the futile flutter of what was not, nor can be, and is everything. Give me more wine, because life is nothing."

"Pessoa," he says to the silence.

And adds, in a louder voice:

"Modern day history is written with memory; and for those of us who choose to forget it, all we have left is the ignoble resource of silence.

It's a lousy defense. But he has no other.

He walks into the dining room, and looks over to where Jorginho is giving instructions to Caími, who goes into the kitchen:

"A bourbon, please, or a whisky, or wine, or whatever you have, it's an emergency."

The two smile.

"Truly, damn it, because life is nothing."

"Isso," says Jorginho, elongating the "I," adding in Portuguese, "Pessoa is right: life is nothing."

"You've read Pessoa?"

"No, but I recite him."

46.

Bruno Fólner writes, as he does almost every morning, facing the sea. The rhythmic crashing of the waves and the soft mellow breeze soothe him and inspire ideas he imagines to be a thousand years old, although he doesn't know what strange magic spell steers his hand over the notebook. The red notebook is small, but a better instrument for writing than the laptop, which is upstairs, in his room, also overlooking the sea.

He looks at his hands and they seem more angular than yesterday. Today they're like the rigid claws of a bird of prey.

He's not angry about getting old, but recognizes a certain uneasiness.

He tends to prefer the sensual feeling of the hand controlling the pencil, the Parker, or a ballpoint pen, transformed into daggers and darts. This produces an exquisite pleasure, unique, and yet beautiful in its reiteration. That mechanical, compulsive gesture leads him to glide the pen over whatever small notebook comes his way, like the kind of local Moleskines you can buy for ten bucks, spiraled or not, made of paper so stiff and rustic they bring about an immense pleasure.

And what if he checks his accounts to see if there's an email from the kids?

The idea baffles him. What's with that, if he doesn't expect anything. And he doesn't want to know anything. I'm dead to them. You don't send letters to the dead.

But how tempting.

Well, what if I just go and take a look, chances are no one's written to me, they know me, they know once I make up my mind . . .

And so why bother checking, it's harmful curiosity, it will just bring me down. If there are messages or not. It's not worth it, even for nothing, I'm setting a trap for myself. Better to write a bit more. Or take a walk. Or keep reading what happens to Jean Valjean, you can't go wrong there. That's it. Hugo prefigures the next century, the struggle between good and bad, and in a rampant, blistering style. Well I think I'm going to look and see if there are emails from the kids, or from Alberto, Lautaro, crazy Elena, who must have heard about it by now. What are they going to say to me, if they say anything at all? Wonderful, dear G.R., merciful, the right thing to do. Or you shitty bastard, how could you, Elena would say to me, life itself calls the shots, or God, or destiny, not you, you son of a bitch messianic murderer.

That's it, I'm not reading a thing. I don't expect a thing, so forget it, besides I closed all my accounts. Enough.

Distraught, he serves himself another cup of coffee and remembers Nelly, the servant from *Wuthering Heights* who recounts the family's story in the manner servant characters narrated a couple centuries ago. What story would Nelly create from this, given she was such a genius for telling the painful affairs of families ruled by tragic relationships?

Then a story comes to mind, that's a tale he's not going to write, certainly not, but he imagines it. The little girl has lost her mother during childbirth, and another Nelly becomes her nanny. The widower yearns for his dead wife with love and abnegation, but he's now had children with another woman and has moved away from the town. He's a highly regarded doctor in the region, and with an honest and virtuous reputation because, in addition to his new family, he keeps the memory of his dead wife alive and provides the little girl with a good education. Everyone, including Nelly, says the girl is the treasure he loves and cares about the most. Naturally the girl, who for years was the joy of the household, grows up and one day falls in love with an unsuitable man. One who is twice her age, with the potbelly of a baker and the disposition of a tarantula. What's more, he abuses her, and before long, turns her into a prostitute. She ends up bearing four children from who knows what fathers, and the scumbag condemns them all to a dreadful life picking through garbage in the city dumps. The story ends when one night, the once beautiful girl, brimming with resentment and hatred, blows his head off with a shotgun loaded with cartridges. Then they arrest her, separate her from her children, condemn her to a life sentence, and once locked up in your typical Argentine prison, infested with filth and violence, she rips a sheet with her teeth, knots it, and hangs herself in a latrine.

"Hovering over the soul, the futile flutter of what was not, nor can be, and is everything," Bruno Fólner recites.

47.

As if propelled by a rocket, he walks all along the bay at dusk, climbs the hill swept by the wind off the Atlantic at that hour, and arrives at a place very close to Zé Antonio's bar. It's a cloudy evening, gray, with turbid waters. Tempestuous seas, he thinks. What a literary century, the nineteenth!

In the *Loja Dona Anna*, which is a kind of large kiosk and cyber center near where he got off the bus, how long ago he no longer knows, Bruno Fól-ner asks to use a computer and sits down to write a letter that of course he doesn't believe he's capable of sending, but he writes it anyway. Then he's going to open his three email accounts, and in whichever one functions, or in all three, he's going to hit Send with the decisiveness of a grenadier.

He addresses it to Marina, and tells her that he's sorry, that he's very sorry, so very sorry, and he doesn't know if she'll ever be able to forgive him. Or rather he knows, and accepts that she'll never forgive him. And that makes sense, he says to himself: how can such a crime be forgiven? You go and kill the girl's mother and then ask her for forgiveness.

And that's all. Or should be. What more can a father who's been ex-pelled from Paradise say? He's now an old man, and he's not sick, but his is a life with a more or less fixed expiration date, and on top of that, weighed down with guilt, this enormous feeling of guilt that presses on his chest, like a steel iron that can't be lifted.

And if perhaps his good health were just an illusion, he certainly wouldn't have the will to try to recover; he's made up his mind that he'll never subject himself to any treatment, no tubes or any of that crap, after all, that's why he did what he did.

My daughter, I've loved you more than anything in the world, he writes. And immediately asks himself if that declaration is enough. Will it suffice? He mulls it over for a few seconds and responds yes to himself, asking what other words he should say. But no, no way, he stops, no, the hell with this mushy crap, there's no way, nothing will be enough. Surely I've been demonized by all in the Chaco. Crime kills happy times. And even though one of them, perhaps Tomi, wouldn't condemn me absolutely, all will carry the wounds, old man, that's for sure, you killed their old lady and it's not an excuse to say now that Sara would've died anyway, inevitably, because that's something only God knows, and look how I've managed to stick God in this mess, the hell with opening emails. And he deletes what he's written, closes the computer, stands up, pays, and leaves, devastated.

48.

"Would *Senhor* Bruno like a *caipirinha*, a beer? Caio asks, approaching politely the table where he's working.

"*Obrigado, filho, não,*" he responds, turning down the kind offer without looking up from the notebook in which he writes. Frustration and pain hold him captive, detaining the movement of his stiff hand, suspended in the air, which then recovers and grasps the pen that glides across the paper like a skier over the calm and clear Totora Lagoon. Not only does the pain cease to subside with the passing days, but it grows, spreading like a plague, bleeding me dry like a vampire. Although it sounds horrible, it has sucked the life out of my soul, and now I have to face the enormous task of saving, protecting, stashing each drop of my blood, each micron of energy, whatever I have left before everything explodes, before a shitty cancer breaks out in my guts like a grenade.

At times, it's as if he can feel it. I detect it, I can confirm its presence like a tapping centipede, first on one side, now on the other, a teeny step here, a teeny step there, a miniscule malignant army, a furtive infectious rat that gnaws on me, sticking in its snout, sucking and sucking, like the poultry mite in Quiroga's "The Feather Pillow."

The murky abyss has no bottom and I peer into its depths; he looks at it and writes that Bruno Fólner looks at it, focused on visualizing with words that unfathomable precipice, that potential infinite journey to the very center of the Earth. He feels fear, an anxious panic that makes his right leg tremble under the table, like Doña Berta, Sarita's mother, who'd pedal the Singer for hours, tirelessly and complaining in Yiddish so that no one could understand her.

That's exactly what he feels now. A slight tremble, a barely restrained sign of fear of death, as if dying could be avoided, something determined by individual choice. The foolishness of that assertion irritates him, and he lifts his gaze and looks out at the boardwalk. What he sees off in the darkness is the faint shimmering glow of the calm waters. At that hour, the sea appears to rest from the constant toil of the day, allowing its surface to become as soft and light as a carpet, or better still, a mirror for the stars. And it's as if he could also see in that darkness the tortured face of Luchi, and that of Norma meditating in the cemetery, the first representing a Greek tragedy and the second a Shakespearian one. And he sees Rejane smiling as she sways to a samba, and Jorginho and Dona Amalia dancing and grinning, and Caio rattling the cocktail shaker and dancing with absolute natural grace to the rhythm of a samba sung flawlessly by Toquinho.

He gives the pen a rest, that is to say, he rests his hand, while he immerses himself in his memories, like one who plunges into the sea at the hour when the marine universe seems to settle down. And observing the charming innkeepers, as Brazilian as the Corcovado or the favelas, he wonders how he'll manage to live, if this is what life will be, how will he be able to live without Sarita, and without Marina and the boys, what did I do, damn it, what did I do…

The guilt fades when he recognizes the unique voice of María Bethânia, a bit husky, crisp and tender, soothing, capable of making one dream that eternal love is possible. Bruno Fólner searches for words to order a drink, a bourbon now, yes, but they don't emerge. Suddenly he feels he can no longer handle his utter confusion. His desertion is so dreadful, the lexical void so immense, the muted hush so complete that for one instant, one second of panic, he believes he'll die from silence. He feels as if he's submerged in a vacuum of words, and besides, I'm tired, he confesses to himself, repressing the desire to go off and cry, or more than tired, exhausted, wiped out like a slow-moving boat that made it through a tsunami and needs a safe harbor. Suddenly, abandonment looms so large, oblivion so deep, so durable the unyielding wall of silence, and he thinks with a bitter smile, the poor little boat makes it to the port, but dies there: rolls over in the harbor, and remains there, forever, keel in the air, ass pointing north.

No one responds to the appeals I don't make, incapable of raising the anchor that ties me to this bay. The lights of Praia Macacos flicker on the hill at night like a shower of cinders, reminiscent of Rejane's hair. And over this way, toward this side of the hill, the open sea in the penumbra, the Atlantic immense and lethal, more sensed than certain, like the lure of suicide. And beyond, more sea, once again the sea, always the sea that encompasses everything.

Please forgive me, my daughter, even if you can't forgive me. That's what I should have written to you. Only that. And he mulls it over for a few seconds and gathers the momentum to rip up what he just wrote, to tear it into bits and pieces, and mince it like an onion on a cutting board.

49.

Since that dawn when he heard the voice of Sarita, the ants haven't returned, as if he'd exterminated them. Suddenly, they disappeared for two days, three, counting those nights, and they haven't come back. That's when Bruno Fólner realizes he's stopped dreaming.

Strange, because he's always dreamed a lot, for years, night after night, and even siesta after siesta. Years ago, he used to joke that he didn't have 365 opportunities to dream like everyone else, but rather 730 because in the Chaco the siesta is sacred, ha-ha. So he wrote *Dreamworld*, a collection of short texts that he called minimalist artifacts, and which the critics ignored completely and was the perfect no-seller.

G.R. used to think back then — Bruno Fólner thinks now — that dreaming isn't worth praising in itself, but at least it doesn't deserve condemnation. And if dreams are the principle source of literature, there's nothing wrong with engineering something that's apparently useless, that doesn't exist for a purpose; constructing something out of what was pure illusion at one imprecise instant; and erecting an ethereal building, perhaps with the only intention of eliciting emotion, evoking nostalgia, or arousing affinities.

Rejane looks at me with sad, clear eyes, intently, as if she were reading my thoughts. A few seconds later, she stands up and walks toward the door and slips out, like one of Verdi's courtesans. A half hour later, when I go down to the dining room, I ask Jorginho if Praia Macacos is a town of readers. Good God, no. But you all know how to read, right? Amalia and I do. Caio doesn't. And Rejane? *Não*, I don't believe so.

50.

That night, Bruno Fólner dreams about his grandmother once again. To say once again means his grandmother appears every now and then, sporadically. Almost always when he's in trouble. She comes naturally to him, like magic, you could say, with him waking up suddenly and seeing her there, in a corner of the room, or next to the window with her back to the garden. Generally this happens shortly before daybreak, and he opens his eyes and discovers her, dressed completely in white, with a full pleated skirt and a dress coat, like the ones they wore a century ago. Now he realizes that she walks with a slight limp, a kind of Waldira from another century, or another world, and who's also lame. She doesn't speak to him, nor can he be certain she looks at him. His grandmother's face always remains in the shadows, like a vague silhouette. On some mornings, he poses a question or comment at times, or asks for advice, but she never responds. She's simply stands there, all dressed in white, with her face hazy and blank, her presence eloquent, and then she disappears.

This happens, Bruno Fólner notes each time, whenever I find myself in trouble with some particular problem, or about to make a difficult decision; or when I'm disturbed and don't know what to do, or how to react. In my house, in the Chaco, she'd remain standing by the window in my bedroom, while now she's in the corner of the room that's also by a large window. My grandmother's attitude is always the same: silent, stern, and somewhat aloof, but attentive to my needs. I know that's how it is, and in those cases, when she appears, I feel a sudden serenity, a definite sensation that something good is going to happen and that everything, finally, will turn out all right. Her presence is always favorable. And for this reason, whenever she appears, I immediately feel some form of relief. That's why I also call out to her sometimes, invoking her in times of need. But in those cases, she never makes an appearance. Everyone knows that characters in dreams do whatever they like. And so my grandmother comes when she likes, or she doesn't come at all, he admits to himself.

That morning, Bruno Fólner wakes up aware that he's dreamed about her, and he sees her there. One could call it a new encounter, serene, calm, without words or gestures, but comforting, soothing. It lasts a few minutes and there's no dialogue, just that intense and eerie gaze. And when she vanishes just before he wakes up, and while he takes the usual long shower under warm water, and later when he goes down to have coffee contemplating the sea, Bruno thinks, as he has other times, that he should write a story about the appearances of his grandmother. Or include her in that novel he seems to be developing, but hasn't yet written, except for some notes.

But he knows he won't do it. He never wanted to include his grandmother in a text, and much less now, so in the future they can't say later that G.R. also ended up writing clichés, magical realism, and all that shit, are you kidding, he says to himself, no fucking way I'm going to use the old woman. Better to let her strange visits occur whenever she likes, let her appear when she appears and in those cases, surely, everything will be like always: tenuous, beautiful and soothing. Like a soft stroke of optimism that the old woman, a specter in white, brings when things turn ugly. That's good enough.

That should be enough, better said. Although now nothing seems to be enough.

51.

One night he asks her, "Why me, I'm old and a foreigner?"

Silence is the response, but a little later she says, "You don't have a past. You don't exist here."

The smell of shrimp sizzling in oil and garlic in a kitchen reaches them.

Everything ends when the other one leaves, Bruno. She looks into his eyes. Marco left one day, and so did I.

You could stay.

One of these days, they'll come for you too. And everything will be memories and *saudades*, longings.

The previous night, like the other nights, with the windows open and the gentle intrusion of a moon beam carried by the sea breeze, she spoiled him like a patient and loving wet nurse. The prolonged encounter of kisses, tongues and fingers culminated in a kind of ceremony of quietude, and, like every time she's visited him, they barely speak, and he goes along for the ride like someone mounting his own bewilderment. Love is rare at this venerable age, says Bruno Fólner to himself, when reality is so petty, and it's not enough to sustain oneself on illusions alone.

Rejane also maintains distance. She revels in delight, in silent concentration, in a profound and silent way, but she never surrenders, nor will she ever. She doesn't want to hurt him or herself. In the middle of the night, every night, she leaves him while he's sleeping, and withdraws furtively, like a phantom. And the next day, every following day, Bruno Fólner awakens, knowing she's not there. Sometimes, before going down for breakfast, he detects, or believes he detects, her presence on the pillow, that faint scent of a woman.

He certainly wouldn't be upset if Rejane settled into the hotel, if he could have her every night, read poems to her, share what he writes as it unfolds, stop the bleeding when he sees her in pain, accompany her on walks along the shore, dance the samba with her, and harmonize with her when she sings softly. Yet he knows these are impossible dreams. How can he imagine they can go off together perhaps to another town, wander in search of elusive security, which now seems threatened ever since Yellow Choppers stuck his nose in his business?

Of course, he shouldn't be so concerned about him. Perhaps it's just a few fireworks going off. Who'd come and look for me? Who'd want to find me? Who, if Bruno Fólner buried G.R. and the dead rest in peace?

Choppers, why not, when at most he's nothing but a swine of an investigator.

Although it's possible he's no longer on my case, it's still disturbing. "*Um destes días...*," one of these days," as Rejane has said.

So what security am I talking about, come on, what am I talking about?

God, I need a double shot of bourbon, or triple, along with a Montecristo to smoke while our wonderful story unfolds, one we'll actually know how to write.

52.

"In the drug world, things change as if by the magic of the mafia, *mafically*," he thinks and smiles at his clever thought. He feels optimistic, like any poet delighted with himself each time a small miracle emerges, and truly the luminous morning contributes to that state of mind.

He smiles before the mirror. After shaving, he slaps his cheeks with La Franco cologne. It's still almost full. He wonders what he's going to do when it runs out. You can't get it in Brazil.

For a fleeting instant, the memory of Luchi and her final screams surfaces, her futile cry for help, and that agony buried inside him forever, perhaps because he never knew if an accusation was also in that plea. He thinks of the twofold horror his sister must have felt over the imminent torture and the ominous cowardice of the family.

Sarita, on the other hand, didn't scream, but when he remembers her, it's as if she were present, and he was seeing her suspended in the air above her hospital bed, screaming like crazy don't kill me, don't kill me, don't kill me...

Distraught, he lights a small cigar and goes over to the window to smoke it. His optimism suddenly goes up in smoke. He needs to get a grip, he thinks, while gazing at the vast enigma of the sea. Rejane he says. She is the sea. He looks at the cigar between his fingers and urges himself to be calm, Bruno, calm down.

Another toke, even deeper. He savors the tobacco. This really is a good thing, to smoke again, but not cigarettes rolled in paper and full of chemicals, rather just a rolled tobacco leaf. He spent years envying smokers, while at the same time trying to convince them to quit smoking, feeling sorry for them, or condemning them, like a typical convert.

He inhales, slowly and with pleasure, and remembers the afternoon when he decided to stop smoking. He still lived in Buenos Aires and was driving down Avenida Córdoba in a little Fiat he called Vittorio. It was rush hour, five in the afternoon, and he was chain smoking like a Black Howler monkey mimicking a human and laughing like an ignorant oaf. Until he felt that stabbing pain in the chest, right in the middle of the sternum, and started to sweat immediately, and everything became blurry. He slowed down, pulled the car over to the sidewalk, and parked as best he could. It seemed like his chest was too small, and the sharp pain spread diagonally, from his right shoulder to his left ribcage.

He told himself he couldn't be so unlucky as to suffer a heart attack right there at that moment, damn, alone like a beggar and unable to drive to the hospital and ask for help. He'd been stressed out for hours and smoking one cigarette after another, so all he could manage to do was throw the butt away, close the car windows, and recline the seat completely to lie back as much as possible. I tried to slow down the tachycardia and took slow breaths, making sure to fill up my lungs. I focused on that, on returning my breathing to normal and did it so thoroughly that I fell asleep. And when a cop woke me up by tapping on the window, it was already night. He asked me if I felt all right, I told him yes, that I was just a little tired, and I started up Vittorio and drove slowly to my apartment, swearing I'd never smoke again. When I got there, the sharp pain in my chest had disappeared, but I could still feel palpitations. Then I took a long shower and afterwards, looking at the Zippo and the Marlboros, I said to them, you shitheads, you're not going to kill me, and I went to bed naked and turned off the light. And that's where they stayed, forever, on the table, the pack of smokes and the lighter.

The cigar he smokes now, looking at the horizon while leaning out the window, as if posing for a painting by Dalí or Matisse, tastes delectable to him. His hands still retain the fragrance of La Franco. He likes the combination of scents that seem to blend with those carried by the sea breeze. He imagines a ship or a rampant train, loaded with bottles of cologne, and he thinks about Calvino. Actually, it's the word that invokes Calvino's *Il barone*

133

rampante. What is it that's rampant? The rampant one climbs, soars. He may be a despicable person, with unlimited ambition. Check out the bastard's claws. Like the lion, he can snag you, hang on and climb, ascend, ravage. He thinks, there's the lofty lion that graces the French coat of arms. Gallic lion. Then he thinks that rampant also means to plead, slither, crawl with the belly over the shitty surface of the world. Might Sarita have pleaded when she felt she could no longer breathe? And might Luchi have crawled at one time to escape?

Enough of this bullshit, Fólner. Enough. That's enough. Period.

And just then there's a knock at the door.

53.

"Dom Bruno...," stammers Jorginho, staring at him intently.

Next to him, Dona Amalia is sad and upset. It seems she came upstairs against her husband's wishes.

"She left, Dom Bruno. She returned to the sea," she said, as if shielded behind Jorginho, and looks straight at him.

Bruno Fólner looks up and furrows his brow, holding their gaze and considering quickly the weight of all the words the innkeepers have uttered. Their quiet reserve is compelling, as if the world had turned into a silent movie.

Dona Amalia sniffs, like someone who moans or cries.

"Her white dress washed up with the tide," she mutters. It's outside there, if you want to see it."

"There's nothing to see," Jorginho grumbles.

Bruno Fólner nods his head, ordering himself to keep a poker face. The couple withdraws, both of them somewhat perplexed by his steady silence.

He feels a kind of intense and immediate fear. He calls it devastation. He looks at his hands. They're trembling.

He goes over to the window and looks at the boardwalk, the beach, the horizon that extends far and wide. Then he knows how much he has loved that sea, that town, those people. He knows he has loved what was confusing because love is confusion, and he also knows that this time has been, perhaps, the season of his last happiness.

54.

At the moment he's about to close the door to go downstairs, without a plan and feeling more bewildered than shaken, Jorginho appears once again on the stairs and stops him.

He looks flustered, worried, and speaks to him with a sense of urgency.

"Two guys who looked like detectives came here," he says, barely moving his lips. When he speaks, his eagle eyes squint, but not out of distrust. "They asked for you, and since I didn't like their looks, I told them you'd gone out sailing very early. They said they'd return."

After alerting him, Jorginho turns around and goes downstairs, as if he had urgent matters to attend to.

The warning sounds absurd and unexpected. Worried and frantic, like never before, Bruno Fólner feels an ominous premonition overwhelming him, tying him down like a gorilla who falls into a trap and struggles to free himself from the ropes. He decides to just go downstairs, even though he doesn't know what for. He leaves the room and heads straight for the stairs, but before the first step, he turns around and goes back, and while retracing his steps in the hallway, as slowly and nonchalantly as he can, his mind racing, he orders himself to hide his anxiousness. He knows he can't, but he gives himself the command. He feels agitated, as if he'd run the four hundred meter — and then he goes back into the room.

He knows, as he knew at all times, that this could happen. It was a given that one day the cops would show up there. They're always snooping around, and there's not a place on earth where a cop can't screw you. And if you're a fool, the heat will always come down on you. If you have no power or useful dirty ties, the heat will close in on you, sooner rather than later.

He feels panic for a few seconds, but then gets a hold of himself. Everything was going well, and he even received that gift called Rejane, phantom or tangible, real or dreamed, a natural wonder of Praia Macacos. There's no reason for anything to change.

But he's very aware that everything's about to change, and in just a few minutes.

So he raises his eyebrows, resigned because, after all, he always knew he was rounding the last turns of a hurdle race, and would end up as wasted as Sarita. So it's the end of the road, old man. They're coming for me now and let's see how I can give them the slip. Turn myself in, not on your life. Not even if they guarantee me it'll be just a question of putting up with a judicial process, a few months in the slammer and public scorn, and then chau, a slow descent into oblivion. But no, not even that, I won't spend one fucking day in jail. And not because I'm courageous, but because I won't. I just won't.

They always come for us. Someone, something, the unexpected, comes looking for you. Never fails.

And you always try to escape. That never fails either.

Quickly, he stuffs a backpack with a change of clothes, a couple books, the Moleskine and the Mac. He wonders if he'll go downstairs again, as he does every morning, but first he peers out the window to check out the day, the sea, which he knows are there waiting for him, as splendid as always, but different now because he notices immediately something's out of place down there. Clearly, oddly, something's off. Parked on the left side of the hotel, next to the bougainvillea that extend toward the sidewalk, there's a patrol car, and on the coastal avenue, from the top of the boardwalk, comes another.

In the same instant, he becomes alarmed and observes that the parked car has its front windows down and is empty, as if its occupants had already gotten out to come up and look for him.

He feels a sudden panic, while all his senses function together on high alert. He runs over to the safe, takes out his passport, the checkbooks, and the money, drops Gordo Núñez's cyanide pill into the back pocket of his pants, and puts on the leather *carpincho* jacket and the straw hat he bought by the sea wall a few days ago, doing everything at record speed. From the night stand, he also grabs the thick volume of *Les misérables* that's he's been rereading. And with a surprising nimbleness impossible for even him to explain, he climbs over the window sill, confirms that the second patrol car is now below, steps outside, closing the window behind him, and walks along the roof with extreme caution so as not to lose his balance.

He circles the building until he can no longer see the ocean, and squats down on a small, low-walled terrace, which looks out only on the blue sky and has a locked door with no handle.

He's certain no one has seen him, but all the same, he barely lifts his head and peeks around. Nothing strange is happening, but he sees there are a dozen people on the beach, and several of them are looking toward the inn, and not, as normal, toward the sea, the waves, the horizon. He ducks immediately and breathes deeply to calm his nerves, waiting for his heart rate to settle down, and nodding his head to muster courage, he retreats a couple meters and rests against the wall, topped by blue roof tiles that lead to an interior patio, and then he grabs the backpack, the Mac, the hat, and slides over the blue tiles to a kind of tiny terrace on the right. There, he walks bent over, keeping his balance with his back against the brick wall, until he finishes circling the building. Then he jumps very carefully onto a load of sheets that he knows are piled by the laundry room door every morning. He lands on his feet with bent knees, with surprising agility for his age, and from there, he runs to hide behind the privet hedge, next to the back street.

He moves swiftly and silently, telling himself there's no guarantee the block's not surrounded, but he's played out, he tells himself, like the gambler who bets everything he has, all or nothing.

On edge and as stealthily as a cat, he creeps forward along the hedge, nearly squatting and in controlled silence, breathing through his mouth, which he keeps open so as not to hear himself panting.

No one peers from any window, no voices can be heard, the garden is empty and only a few plants sway in the fresh sea breeze. The pool looks placid, blue and serene, and the umbrellas are still collapsed from the night before. João, who takes care of the pool and garden, hasn't shown up yet, even though it's after nine.

Bruno Fólner imagines the dialogue that must be unraveling between Jorginho, Dona Amalia, and the cops, who are surely a pair, just as surely as another pair is outside and others on the corner and on the street along the boardwalk. They always come in pairs, and if there are more, you're shit out of luck.

He surveys the back street once again and sees they're lined up, on the two corners, facing the inn, with their backs to the bay. A Pousada da Baleia is surrounded, and inside all seems empty and quiet. It's Wednesday, cloudy outside, the circle closed, all siren lights blazing, and fear, or perhaps what isn't fear but really seems like it, negates all other thoughts. Then he makes up his mind and enters the kitchen through the service door, quite naturally.

Jorginho and Dona Amalia have just entered as well, and look at him as if everything were normal, but fear and wariness can be detected on their faces. Bruno Fólner raises his index finger to his mouth and places the heavy backpack, the thick book, the Mac, the jacket, and the hat on the floor, and instantly the kitchen is transformed into a silent and somber temple.

He spies through the pass through window and sees two guys, unmistakably cops, one looking toward the stairs and the other toward the boardwalk. He sees a third, in uniform, on the sidewalk. Your typical pack of hounds, Bruno Fólner says to himself, silent and on guard.

He looks at Jorginho, who also looks at him, intently, with his eagle eyes.

Bruno Fólner takes the envelope full of dollars out of the backpack and places it on the table.

"In case I run into problems," he murmurs, staring at the innkeeper, "this is for both of you, okay?"

Jorginho blinks and barely raises his eyebrows, his only gesture of understanding. But he takes the envelope, inside which Bruno Fólner has left many more dollars than what his bill at the Inn of the Whale adds up to.

"You have anything to drink around here?"

"There's always something," Jorginho says, and he takes out a bottle from under the kitchen counter, as if he were a magician.

Bruno Fólner smiles, not without a tinge of bitterness, and thinks, clear and serene, that anyway it was beautiful being there, that he'll miss them, and when the time comes, any hour is good if you know, for certain, it's your last moment of happiness.

"They went upstairs to look for me and the other two are over there, right?" and he points toward the dining room.

Jorginho nods yes ever so slightly with his head. He's so sad it seems he's about to cry.

"Are they over there, and upstairs and outside?"

Jorginho purses his lips and nods, his eyes brimming with tears. Dona Amalia whimpers aloud, quietly.

Bruno Fólner empties the glass with one gulp, accepting that there's no way out. Nor does he want to continue to flee, or to face anything. He's seized by a sudden feeling of weariness he believes to be eternal. He concedes he's overwhelmed, worn out. Life can also leave you exhausted. If well-lived, he corrects himself, and I don't have complaints, not too many. You played your cards. One last move.

Then he takes the pill from the back pocket of his pants and looks at it, as if with innocent curiosity. As if he'd just found it. Or as if it were an object of investigation to be examined. He smiles slightly, with fear, but above all, feeling desolate, and he puts it in his mouth, bites it, swallows it, and washes it down with another whisky. His smile lingers, as if clinging to some point on the wall. Or in the air. Or in the memory of no one.

Charlottesville — Resistencia, 2012–2015.

The Author

Mempo Giardinelli was born in Resistencia, capital of the Chaco province in Argentina on August 2, 1947. He is an award-winning author of novels, short stories, essays, and children's fiction, and a journalist, and founder of La Fundación Mempo Giardinelli. He lived in exile, in Mexico (1976–1984), where his first works of fiction were published. He has taught Latin American literature at universities in Argentina, Mexico, and the United States, and been honored as a Doctor Honoris Causa by universities in France, Paraguay, Argentina, and Mexico.

Giardinelli has garnered many prestigious awards for his works of fiction and essays, among them the Premio Rómulo Gallegos (1993), which is the most important literary award in the Spanish-speaking world. His works have been translated to twenty-six languages and are the subject of critical articles, dissertations, and books published in Argentina and other South American countries, the United States, and Europe.

The Translator

Rhonda Dahl Buchanan is a professor of Spanish and the director of the Latin American and Latino Studies Program at the University of Louisville. She has translated the narrative fiction of the Argentine writers Ana María Shua, Perla Suez, Tununa Mercado, and Mempo Giardinelli, and the Mexican writer Alberto Ruy Sánchez, among others, and is the author of numerous critical studies on contemporary Latin American writers. Her translation of three novels by Perla Suez, *The Entre Ríos Trilogy,* was published in 2006 by the University of New Mexico Press in their Jewish Latin America Series. She is the recipient of a 2006 NEA Literature Fellowship for the translation of Alberto Ruy-Sánchez's novel *The Secret Gardens of Mogador: Voices of the Earth* (White Pine Press, 2009). Her translation *Quick Fix: Sudden Fiction* by Ana María Shua, an illustrated anthology of microfictions, was published in 2008 by White Pine Press. In 2014, White Pine Press published her translation *Poetics of Wonder: Passage to Mogador* by Alberto Ruy-Sánchez, with support from Mexico's PROTRAD translation program. Her translation of Perla Suez's novel *La Pasajera* was published as *Dreaming of the Delta* in 2014 by Texas Tech University Press, with the support of Argentina's translation program, Programa Sur. In 2019, White Pine Press published her translation, *The Devil's Country,* a novel by Perla Suez.